INKSTAINS

January

John Urbancik

InkStains
January
John Urbancik

For more information, please visit www.darkfluidity.com

ISBN: 0692356347
ISBN-13: 978-0692356340 (DarkFluidity)

For everyone who has ever
touched a pen to paper.

ACKNOWLEDGMENTS

It would've been impossible to write all these stories by hand without the help of Cross fountain pens and all the notepads I used – including Moleskine, Lechtturm1917, and Rhodia – none of whom provided me with any promotional considerations.

As I took this journey, and twisted my hand into unrecognizable distortions, Mery-et suffered the most even as she gave me her full support. Thank you.

And thanks, as always, to Sabine and the Rose Fairy.

Inkstains January

January

John Urbancik

INTRODUCTION

When I started this project, I aimed to write a story every day for a year. By hand. I found an inexpensive yet fancy fountain pen (fountain pens are, by definition, fancy), started with a Moleskine notepad, and on 1 January 2013 set to writing.

I allowed myself three days off per month; after a few months in which I only took one day, I decided to make it one day – a mandatory day, at that – through the rest of the year.

Stories did not have to be fiction. Nonfiction, essays, reviews, memoirs – all genres – everything was open to me, so long as they were complete.

These are the results: failures and successes both. I made zero editorial decisions on what to include. I cleaned up grammar and spelling, and spent months typing up the almost 250,000 handwritten words; I did my best to strengthen the writing where it was weak. I'm very happy with a lot of the stories, and disappointed with others, but I think some are fantastic. (I'm biased. You decide.)

As these InkStains collections come out one month at a time, I invite you to follow me on this journey. See where I went. You'll start to recognize recurring themes. You'll start to wonder why I'm so fascinated with a nursery rhyme. You'll start to map out your own journey. You'll know, almost to the day, when I went to New Orleans; but will you know when I went to New York, or where else I might have gone?

As you read this year's writing, I'm doing it again. I've embarked on another InkStains project. The twist, for 2015, is that I will decide on a monthly theme to unify the stories – whatever they may be.

JANUARY

Welcome to the first month of the year. You are welcome to read a story every day – every day but the one I took off – to follow my progress naturally. You are just as welcome to devour them in an entire night.

In January we'll see fast cars and old gods, magic and myth, the first of my maps – a theme I'll return to throughout the year – a few dangerous women, and the birth of poetry. I hope you enjoy following my journey.

1 JANUARY

The moon overhead: she smiles on me, she guides me, she offers me the greatest of gifts, even if I cannot recognize them at the time.

The moon, high above, sends her blessings, sends her archers, sends her poisonous children to aid me in the great things I must – in this lifetime – accomplish.

The moon, behind her veil or fully exposed, doesn't merely watch. She manipulates. She plans. She changes. She's responsible for the most intricate machinations.

The moon, hanging low, tonight, eyes – angry, disappointed, dissatisfied – focused on me. She's taken her blessings, she's sent her archers and poisons, she means to eradicate me.

I won't let her.

I have learned a great many things and fostered a great many talents. As fine as her archers may be, I am swift, agile, light as the wind, and fluid like no thing these men have ever seen.

Arrows in the air, a rain of them – a storm, but I retreat to city streets and narrow alleys. I force them to chase me into close quarters. They are archers, designed for long range assault, and have little protection from my knives.

I don't make them suffer. I am quick and merciful, merely fighting for my life, my own life, and perhaps the fate of the world. I don't know if I'm bold enough to make such an assertion.

Ultimately, the moon's archers fail, and the moon's archers fall.

I have devoted myself to the study of a great many poisons. The powders do not tempt me. The smokes dissipate. The odorless, colorless, invisible and undetectable poisons she sends – the moon up in her sky – swim uselessly in my veins. They fight amongst themselves, acting and counteracting; and yes, they make me ill, they bring a sickly color to my cheeks, and they steal my strength, but they fail to bring me down. My lungs still draw breath. My heart beats. In an uncomfortable, unsightly moment, I am purged.

Almost, I admit, the venom of a lover threatens me, but even against impossible beauty I emerge triumphant. I would like to say I changed my lover's heart, that *Love* conquered, but this night; alas, that would be a lie.

Finally, atop a hill, within sight of both the city and my former lover's fresh grave, the moon comes down from the sky wrapped in elegant darkness, shadows cascading from her hair, eyes like diamonds, lips and hips dangerously curved.

We circle each other on the hilltop. I can defeat her archers and her poisons, her plans and designs. I can overcome the loss of her favor. I do not know if I am capable of defying the moon directly.

"Why will you not die?" she asks.

"I will. But not tonight."

"Why must you resist me?" she asks.

"I never have."

"You mock me."

"Never would I dare."

She smiles. It's the sharpest weapon in her arsenal. She says to me, "I may have fallen in love."

I don't presume, so I say nothing.

"You have proven yourself worthy," she tells me. She steps forward. I step back. Her smile trembles.

I say, "You turned away from me."

"Tis my nature," she says.

"You set your archers on me, and your poisons."

She shrugs. "I have more archers, and more poisons."

"You wanted me dead."

"Death," she says, "is not an end."

"I will not die this night," I tell her. "I will not fall for your lies, your machinations, your fabrications. I will not fall for you. You'd be gone within a fortnight."

She looks away. A moonlit tear slips from her eye. Sorrowfully, she admits, "Tis my nature." Then she looks to me again and extends a hand, one last, final invitation. "But I promise a glorious fortnight."

2 JANUARY

The crow said to me, "It's time."

I glanced at my $23,000 watch (don't judge me; I'm in the midst of a fever dream) and asked, "Time for what?"

"To float down the river."

"Styx? No." I said it flatly. "That's not going to happen."

"A different river," the crow said. Then with a mighty caw, it flew away, leaving me on this raft without an oar, leaving me to the mercy of the merciless river. I floated, swiftly and with apparent determination (no, I shouldn't really call it floating) until the raft got caught up in the bend of the river.

I'm no raftsman. I've never been on a river. I don't know how they work, except in the grip of a fever dream.

Upon the shore, the land, the dry stuff that surrounded the river, I met a coyote – a desert creature, I'm sure, but you can't blame me. The coyote said to me, "It's time."

"It's not."

"You're already late," the coyote said.

"Then I'll need a faster car."

The coyote grinned the way you'd expect a wolf to grin, then he led me to a sleek, low, red piece of art from Italy on the edge of a long, narrow road.

"Straight on till sunset," the coyote told me.

Let me tell you now, that car was fast. I didn't have to hit the gas to make it go; I had to hold it back with all my weight on the brake just so it wouldn't take off before I was ready.

The road led to a castle. The sweet Italian stallions got me to it in no time.

At the door, a butler greeted me. He called me Lord something, and it might've been my name. He said to me, "The party has already begun."

"They couldn't wait?"

"No, my Lord, the could not."

So I entered the ballroom, where I thought I'd heard all the music, but it was empty. I found a kitchen large enough to cook for the entire Velvet army, but it was hollow and full of the echoes of my footfalls. I found a bathroom with an Olympic sized tub, a jetted tub, the water streaming – but I found no party.

I did find a mouse. The mouse said to me, "It's time."

"We've been over this already, "I told the mouse. "It's not time till I say it's time."

The mouse said again, "It's time."

I gave the mouse a good view of my back.

Somewhere, there was a clock. I imagined it was huge and elegant and gothic, because that's the way it sounded as it struck, struck, struck. I followed the sound until the last of it faded, but never found the source. Yes, I counted the chimes. Twelve. Midnight. Don't assume it means anything, not in the confines of a fever dream.

"There's no party," I said to no one.

A long hall led me a long way, but I made no progress; and though I made no turn, I found myself lost, if not forgotten.

That's when I remembered. I'd drunk from the river, not the Styx, not death, but the other: Lethe, the river of forgetting. I'd given up my memories of me and you and everything. Don't ask me why. I can't remember. Not while in the maelstrom of a fever dream.

I said, "I need it back," though there was no one there to hear.

I responded myself. "You must have done it for a reason."

"No reason is worth sacrificing yourself."

"You're still you."

I had a point, I suppose, but I had another as well: without knowledge of who I was, without my own experiences to guide me, without my past mistakes from which I might learn, was I really me at all? Was I anyone? Or was I merely trapped in the eddies of a fever dream?

I left the house. At the door, the butler said to me, "Leaving so soon, Lord?"

"I must," I told him. "I'm late."

The car, as it turned out, moved just as quickly in the opposite direction.

The coyote, still grinning as a wolf might, agreed to watch the car when I left it, though I doubted I'd ever see it again.

I dove into the river. I couldn't make the raft float against the current, but I had arms and legs and a certainty — without a memory to back it up – that I could swim. I struggled for breath. I reached a familiar shore, the first of my short memories, and as I climbed onto the land the crow returned.

"It's time," the crow said to me.

"Don't rush me," I said.

The water of the river dripped off me. Speckled bands of sunlight through the trees dried me slowly. Eventually, I began to remember – not in a flash of sudden knowledge, but easily and gradually and peacefully, until I even recalled what had driven me into the river in the first place.

Bathed in that memory, tortured in a fever dream, I wept. Every tear returned the fragment of another memory, either good or bad, pieces of my own cloth, my soul, the truth of myself as if escaping a fever dream.

Somewhere, somehow, as my tears slowed, I found an epiphany, something about a whole being made up of fragments of dreams, fever dreams, feverishly me, no longer a blank slate if ever I was.

Sometime after, I woke, not yet recovered but wondrously healed.

3 JANUARY

The rain waits on the horizon, promising and threatening and posturing, darkening the clouds, but held in place by the will of one man.

Marvin is a magician.

He's not particularly good, he's not talented, and he's incredibly lacking in wit and wisdom. He is an aging man with gray hair and a Salvation Army suit, a widower and a veteran, and maybe something of a poet in some deep, rarely tapped crevasse in his heart, but he has learned three tricks of magic. He can pull objects out of a hat, though his isn't a magician's top hat but the kind of Fedora Bogart used to wear. He can always pull the Jack of Spades out of a deck of cards at will. And he can delay the weather.

It's actually a rather simple trick, if taxing. If you asked, he'd gladly teach you. No one has ever asked.

He stands, at the far corner of a parking lot some hours before nightfall, and stares at the billowing clouds, concentrating, breaking a sweat. A crowd gathers around him, jostling each other, murmuring, some deep in the throes of disbelief. He wipes his forehead with the back of his hand. He licks his lips. He glances at the woman with the pale eyes and the blue dress.

"Anyone can do what you're doing," she says. "Don't hold it back. Don't keep it away. Bring it. Bring it in its fullest fury. Bring the rain and the wind and the thunder."

"Now?" he asks.

"Now."

The first drops of rain hit the asphalt. After a brief scattering, it's a deluge. Lightning shatters the sky. The wind whips her dress around her legs. She's smiling. She says, "Unleash it."

Thunder explodes around them. The crowd scatters. The raindrops fall like hail, heavy and cold and solid. The flashes of lightning provide a near-constant flickering. They're already drenched to the bone.

The woman with the pale eyes and the blue dress steps closer to Marvin the magician. The storm has brought color to her cheeks, vibrancy and vividness she'd lacked earlier. She has to shout to make herself heard over the storm. "Keep it going. Keep it ferocious. But keep us out of it."

He grimaces. That's a lot to ask for. But it's a lot of woman to impress, so he nods once and conjures the commands, incites the incantations in his head, tricks the trick into working for him.

Lightning comes down in walls around them; a Faraday cage of air divides them from the world. You can't stop the thunder, which is raucous and exuberant and beyond reason, but the wind winds around them and the rain pummels the ground at their sides. In their wall of lightning and wind, they are protected from the elements.

It's the smallest ever Eye of a Storm. The effort is great. Marvin's sweat is cold and running, his muscles sore and straining. A headache is forming behind his eyes. He sees stars.

The woman with the pale eyes and the blue dress is smiling. She steps closer. He allows the lightning wall to tighten behind her.

"This," she says, "what you're doing, what you're capable of – is absolutely amazing."

Then she kisses him.

It's a good, long, deep kiss, and nothing else matters, so Marvin forgets what he's doing. And the storm, though it calms, blankets them again.

The effort of the magic, the soulfulness of the kiss combine in Marvin's body. He stumbles, and he falls, and he passes out completely.

While he's blacked out, the woman with the pale eyes and the blue dress rummages through his pockets. She steals his pocket watch and a few loose dollars. She takes his fedora, from which he can pull things, and puts it on her head.

She leaves the deck of cards and its eager Jack of Spades. She learned long ago never to rob anyone of everything.

When he opens his eyes, she's gone with his money, his watch, and his hat. But he's still got his cards, so it's not a total loss. And he can still taste her kiss, so it was worth it.

4 JANUARY

There was no such thing as fear. He didn't believe in it. He was fifteen years old, and not one single thing he'd ever feared had done him the slightest bit of harm.

He'd been afraid of the dark, which turned out to by mysterious and magical and alluring, but rarely dangerous and never fatal.

He'd been afraid of the wolves and the bears and even the raccoons, anything in the woods with a mind of its own and the slightest hint of hunger. Ultimately, he'd been hungry once or twice himself. Further, no creature had ever devoured him.

He'd been afraid of a great many things that never came to pass or, in fact, had merely been things unknown. It was stupid to fear a thing you didn't know.

There's no such thing as fear. He said this several times in the mirror, perhaps to convince his reflection, perhaps just to hear his voice break the silence.

The mirror, however, stared back and offered no words of courage, no wisdom, no advice. It merely gave back whatever he gave it.

Right. Fear was a myth. He took a deep, soul-fortifying breath, and strode out of the bathroom with a display of courage and confidence.

There is nothing to fear. There is no fear. Fear itself.

Be afraid. Be very afraid.

His heart had a way of telling his head to take a bath.

He did not falter. Until he rounded the corner and saw her in the hall, near her locker, a book in hand and another inside, he didn't even hesitate.

She looked at him as she shut her locker. She said nothing, but waited for him.

He said her name. Still, she waited.

He said, "I'm sorry."

There. It was out. Two words, little simple things, tiny but far from meaningless. Not exactly what he'd intended, but in a pinch, he thought they were pretty damn good.

"I know," she said. "So am I."

He had hoped for something else, something more forgiving, but it wasn't forthcoming. Perhaps fear was a real thing after all.

In front of the judge, a kid not much older, the prosecutor, one of the girls, said, "He waited too long."

"Is this true?" the judge asked.

He hung his head. "It is."

"You confess?"

"I throw myself at the court's mercy."

"This court knows no mercy."

They stripped him to his underwear and paraded him through the gymnasium and the auditorium. They pronounced his failures and his shortcomings. They declared him foolish, guilty, stupid, naïve, but also brave. In the end, yes, he was brave.

He re-worked his words. He ignored the court in his head. He stopped the girl from walking away by throwing a few more words at her. "I like you."

"I know," she said. She smiled. She kissed his cheek. "Thank you."

He had hoped for something else, something more reciprocal, but it wasn't forthcoming. Perhaps fear was a real thing after all.

In the middle of the stadium, on the mound, surrounded by seventy thousand cameras and flashing bulbs and microphones, he held out his arms and closed his eyes. He screamed to the masses, "I have faced your demons! I have borne your burdens! I have faltered, I have stumbled, but I have not died!"

Perhaps fear was a real thing, but there was no need for it.

He tried to rearrange his words again, tried to prevent the girl from going. A question. He threw out a question. Plucked it from the air. Presented it on the palm of his hand. Questions required answers.

"Would you go out with me?"

"On a date?" she asked, throwing the question right back at him, spiking it, going for the gold.

There was nothing to do but answer it. As careful as he was, this was where he lost control. This was where he slipped. "Yes, on a date. Something nice and simple. I don't have a car, I can't take you someplace far away. And I haven't got much money, I'm not out of High School yet. Neither are you. And I know nothing about Love. I'm still a child, but I'm willing to learn. I'm anxious to learn. I'm a good, good learner. And I do know something about Romance, because I've read a lot of poetry and my father taught me respect and my mother taught me gentleness. I'm strong enough and fast enough, and I am brave, and I believe a girl like you might teach me something of Love. No – not a girl *like* you, no one like you would do. You, and only you, and no one else at all, have stolen all the faces in my dreams and replaced them with yours."

Before the end, he realized he should stop. He tried to stop, but couldn't. There was no helping it. And a crowd had gathered, albeit a small one, but word of his soliloquy would spread fast.

She smiled at him and said, "Thank you." Then she said, "No." Then she walked away.

Surrounded by the firing squad, blindfolded, offered one last cigarette, he refused. "Just shoot," he said.

But no one fired. The crowd broke apart. His story, distorted and twisted right from the start, began to snake its way through the school.

When he turned, there was another girl, pretty and shy like him, but brave enough not to believe in fear. She said, "You were wrong."

He faltered. "How?"

She looked away and said, "Maybe you can learn something of Love with me."

5 JANUARY

Through the dark streets, avoiding streetlamps, slipping between shadows – it's not a living thing, per se, but a thing with intention nonetheless. It cannot be caught by a passing headlight. It is not revealed in the flash of a match.

Three boys at the corner, smoking, drinking, laughing, hiding when the cop rolls by, they don't see it though they hear something, or at least sense it, but they're too young or too weak to pay it much heed.

The young mother, alone in her apartment with a glorious view of the Dumpster in the alley, glances out her window, catches something in the corner of her eye. But the baby is demanding, and demanding now, and there's no one else to help so it's all her and the baby and the baby's needs, nothing else.

The cop, circling the street with his fancy computer and radio and department-issued firearm, he sees nothing except what he expects to see.

The taxi driver who doesn't speak the language but knows every secret of these streets, he most certainly sees it, and maybe he recognizes it, but he says nothing to anyone. No one else here speaks Czech. And even if they did, his job is to provide an illusion of safety, not shatter that illusion.

It's a tough corner in a rough neighborhood on the outskirts of a rough city. Expectations are low. Hope, though it exists, is a commodity to be traded, sold, lost, or forgotten.

Through the narrow alley, through the narrow basement window, up the narrow stairs – it glides as though on a mission. It is ancient, older than language, sometimes hungry, sometimes generous, sometimes merely bored – just as it is bored tonight.

It shifts form, taking substance, creating an illusion of humanity, though it is easy to see through. The demanding cries of the baby attract its attention. It reaches the young mother's door. It takes on solidity. It knocks three times, like a ghost might.

The young mother answers, baby in hand, chain preventing the door from moving more than a few inches. Certainly, no man could just slip through. Her hair is unkempt: dark crescents droop from her eyes. "What is it?" she asks. She's tired. She's always tired.

He smiles unnaturally and says, "I can help." His voice, if nothing else, betrays him. He's no man, he's not human, and his definition of words aren't necessarily in line with words' actual definitions. When he says he can help, he means he can ease the young mother's burden by removing it. Then she could sleep again, and maybe buy new clothes, maybe go back to school and get a decent job and escape this rough neighborhood.

His intentions are transparent.

"I don't need your help," she says, and she tries to shut the door both politely and firmly.

The crack allowed by the chain is not too thin. He slips through it before she can close the door. He reaches for the baby with one hand, her cheek with the other.

The young mother screams.

In a neighborhood like this, screams are not uncommon, but there are many different types. In all the world, in all of history, there have been but a dozen screams of such deep desperation, such a magnitude of vibrant panic, they stopped a thing that might be called a god. While this scream, this mother's cry of naked fear and defiance and fury, was near to that dozen in its tenor, it failed to stop a thing that might be called a god.

It was hungry *now*.

The scream echoed through the apartment building, which was as good as empty. It leaked into the alley and spilled onto the street corner. The bottle of beer in one of the boy's hands shattered.

They responded immediately. They followed the source of the scream into an apartment where the front door should've denied them access. Up to the third floor, to the door of the young mother, ajar but still chained. The baby, in the arms of a thing that looked like a man but might be called a god, wailed like any baby forcibly separated from its mother.

She lay on the floor, unconscious perhaps, or maybe dead, with a trickle of blood above her eye.

The boys knew the mother. The boys knew the baby. The boys did not know the thing holding it. They broke through the door easily. The fault was not in the chain but in the rotted wood. They confronted the baby snatcher. They encircled it. They were confident, because they were youthful and strong and had numbers on their side.

They were foolish.

The first, the thing that might be a god tossed out the window. Glass shattered, but the rusted fire escape held.

The second, the thing that might be a god threw against the living room wall, which had always been thin, into the vacant adjacent apartment. There was nothing but floor and freshly torn drywall to break his fall.

The third, the thing that might be a god carried out the front door. It held the boy with one hand and used him as a battering ram, smashing him first against the broken door and then the wall in the hall. Then it dumped him down the stairs. Several bones cracked along the way.

The young mother opened her eyes. She climbed shakily to her feet. She chased the thing carrying her baby down the stairs and out onto the street.

There, the cop waited with his gun drawn. "Enough," he said, calling upon all his authority and courage and bravado. He'd secretly hoped for a moment in which he might play hero. His department-issued firearm felt warm and anxious in his hand. The baby cried.

The thing that looked like a man and might have been a god cocked his head and blinked his eye and, without moving, snatched the gun from the cop's hands, twisted the metal, and dropped it to the street. He said, "You might hurt the baby."

The cop drew a second, non-standard firearm, which he probably should not have carried, and fired one perfectly placed shot between the eyes. The baby, still crying, was never in danger.

Neither was the thing that might've been a god. He absorbed the bullet, crushed the second gun and, with it, the bones in the cop's hands.

Then he walked away, into the street, and into the path of an available taxi. The driver didn't need language to know not to touch the brakes.

The crash did more damage to the taxi than the thing that looked like a man, but every bit of momentum in the whole of the universe has consequences. The thing that might've been a god dropped the baby.

This time, the young mother's scream was more desperate, more anguished, than any scream in the history of screaming. The boys, also emerging from the apartment, added their horrified gasps. The cop shouted the most heinous series of expletives imaginable. The taxi driver cursed once in his native tongue. It was the most appropriate word he had.

The dropped baby did not land on the steaming hood of the taxi or the dark asphalt street or the cracked sidewalk. The baby did not fall into the gutter. The thing that look like a man and might have been a god moved with a god's speed and a god's gentleness, to catch the baby as quickly as he had dropped it.

For a moment, all was still. This rough corner in a rough neighborhood on the outskirts of a rough city fell preternaturally silent.

The thing that might've been a god kissed the baby's forehead, a blessing of a sort, and returned the baby to the young mother's arms. He said, "I truly meant to help."

"Help some other way," she said.

The thing dissolved into something less solid, less real, and less visible. It slipped away, into the shadows in the alley, away from streetlamps and moonlight. It went away, and it was no longer bored.

It had done some damage. In the days that followed, flowers bloomed in the gutter, the streetlamps at that corner brightened, the cop found his picture on the front page of the newspaper's local section, the boys received scholarships for colleges they hadn't dreamt of applying to, the taxi driver met a woman from Prague who spoke his language – and that woman was, in fact, the young mother. Their romance, after all, was inevitable.

As to the baby, who had benefited from a scream more honest any it could have affected, became satisfied and quiet and curious and quite capable. The baby grew up to be strong and smart and daring. The baby grew up and discovered things, changed things, created things – and ultimately, the baby grew up to destroy things. The baby's name was Adam, and Adam had a wicked future in front of him.

6 JANUARY

Speed. Speed is important. If you can't get there swiftly, you might as well not go. On the ground, you need a car – and it's best to be limited by obstacles, whether still or rolling, than by your own engine. If you haven't got the horses, get off the racetrack.

That red car there, with its five gears and seven liters and twelve cylinders, with its six hundred and something horses, is *fast*. It hugs the corners. It gets you there. Your shadow will have to catch up in its own time.

Go on, take a seat. Enjoy the leather in that cockpit, grip the gear shift, grit your teeth. It's not like you'll get another chance. Check the gauges, crank up a heavy blues beat, and drop that thing into gear.

Don't you love the smell of rubber burning? A heavy kick on that gas now, this is no time to be timid. You're controlling a piece of art, modern art, man and machine, style and substance. *You can go faster than that.*

It's open road ahead of you for a hundred miles or more. The other cars, they'll get out of your way. This is real highway driving, babe. There ain't a thing to slow you down. Foot to the floor now. That's it. Kick it up a gear. Make that thing scream.

Sirens? Don't be stupid. You're a god now, a god of speed, you don't answer to flashing lights. They can't catch you. One ten, one twenty, one thirty. *Faster*, babe. You only live once.

Yeah, those are clouds behind you, and they're bringing rain, but you can outrace the storm, you can leave the world behind. Speed. You're pure energy. One sixty. One seventy. Don't get shy now. It's only a bend in the road. Don't you like the way the tires grip the asphalt? That's not a lot of smoke. *You can go faster.* It's practically a straight line.

One eighty. You're getting brave. I like what I see. I like the music of that engine and the heavy rhythm pounding out of those speakers. Loud music always goes with speed. One ninety. You're pushing it now. Just a little more. Coax those horses over the edge.

Helicopter? So what? It's up in the air. You're on the ground, on the street, a flash of lightning, two hundred miles per hour and they haven't got a chance in Hell of catching you. At least until you run out of gas.

Until then, drive it like you stole it, babe. 'Cause after, you're headed for a long slow stay in a cell.

7 JANUARY

They chased her into a dark dead-end alley. Her name was Simone. When she turned to face her pursuers, an angry mob, she grinned. There was nothing jovial about her expression. It was pure hunger.

I'd warned them.

The mob was about a dozen deep, men mostly, who might have convinced themselves they'd seen something. They hadn't. Not yet.

Simone crouched like a tigress. She said, "Stop," but they did not listen. She did not plead; it wasn't her life at risk. She drew a long, thin blade from the sheath on her hip. She held it defensively. Poison gleamed on its edge.

They came at her anyway.

After she finished with them, when all that remained were steaming corpses and a few final agonized moans, she returned the knife to its home and spoke to me in the shadows. "You've been following me."

"Watching, yes," I admitted.

"You want to know if it's true, what they say about me."

I would've smiled for her if I were capable. "I know that it is."

Another night, I had seen her talking with a rat, stroking its head, giggling, certain they were alone.

Another night, I had seen her accept free bread from the stingy baker. He'd slept every day and night since, and slept still, though I didn't think she knew this.

Another night, I'd seen her drink whiskey from a bottomless bottle.

"You want something," she said.

"We all want something."

"You're not good at enigmatic," she told me.

I stepped out of the shadows so she could see my scars. "I want justice."

"You seek vengeance," she said. "It's not the same thing."

"It's close enough."

"You want my blessing?" she asked.

"I want your dagger and your poison."

She touched the blade sheathed at her hip. "It acts swiftly."

The mob had gone silent. I said, "I know."

She didn't ask who had scarred me or how or why. She didn't ask if there had been another victim, perhaps a mother, a daughter, a lover. She judged me by the expression in my eyes and the determination in my voice. I was unwavering and unafraid. She unhooked the sheath from her hip and handed it over.

I drew the blade, sheath still in hand, and examined the edge. She'd wiped it clean, but there were traces of blood, and of course the poison.

"Return it to me here," she said, "twenty-four hours from now." The threat was implied. I nodded. I left her to her shadows.

My plan had been simple. Twenty-four hours later, precisely, I sat cross-legged in my bare room in the dark.

My boots were next to me, the knife and its sheath in front of me on the ground.

Simone entered through the window behind me. I only head her because she allowed it. I knew she would find me. I knew she'd know my name and, by now, my story.

"My blade is dry," she said. She hadn't even retrieved it. "You failed to find your justice."

"Justice moves at its own speed," I told her.

"You couldn't find him."

"I didn't look."

She knelt in front of me, slid the knife from its leather. The blade glinted. Though dry, it was still potent. "Don't feel bad," she said. "Many who quest for vengeance find they haven't the stomach for it."

"He's dead," I told her.

She raised an eyebrow. She put the knife in its sheath. "How?"

I raised my hands before me, palms up, fingers splayed. "I crushed his windpipe until he could breathe no more."

"Then why the knife?" she asked.

"Comfort."

She went out the way she entered. Twenty-four hours later, in a spice shop, I met Simone again. She had bewitched the shopkeeper; he would never put two coherent words together again. She carried a basket full of garlic and rosemary and salt. She said, "This is no coincidence."

"No."

"You court death."

"You won't kill me," I told her.

"How can you be so sure?"

I didn't answer. I showed her my empty palms. "Teach me."

"Blades?"

"Secrets."

"Poisons?"

"Spells."

She put the knife in my belly. She whispered, "I'll teach you death."

I kissed her. She'd come close enough. She'd done it to herself. The touch of my lips on hers was brief, but it was enough. She drew back. She cursed. She dropped the blade on the floor.

"I'd found my justice long ago," I told her, though it was not an explanation. "Now, it's just for money."

She dropped to her knees. She foamed at the mouth. My poisons, like hers, were swift. She tried to cast a spell, but I'd taken that from her, as well.

My wound would heal. What's one more scar? And it hadn't taken me long to devise a counter for her poison of choice once I knew it.

Simone stopped breathing and her heart stopped beating and she died. I went out to collect the bounty.

8 JANUARY

When a thousand little gods still walked the earth, when humanity was young and the land fresh, before the ages of silicon or iron or bronze, there was a youth in love.

Even then, when there was little worth fighting for, when language was new and inept and inexact, there were few things more worth fighting for than love.

The youth wrestled a bull until it had to yield. The youth diverted the course of a river. The youth dug a hole straight through the mountains with his bare hands.

The girl did not notice.

Let me tell you about the girl. You may have heard of Helen, for whom a thousand ships were launched. You may be familiar with Cleopatra. You might have seen filmic images of Brigitte Bardot. But you have never seen beauty such as existed in her face. There has never been so great a beauty.

She was smart. She knew all the stories. If there had been books, she would have read them all. Until she saw the shapes of unicorns and dragons in the clouds, no one saw anything but cloud. She wore a piece of jade around her neck, which she had found and fashioned herself; before then, no one had ever made jewelry. She discovered salt on a breezy afternoon, discovered pepper over a long weekend. Had there been weaving, she would have woven. Had there been canvasses, she would have painted, and her paintings would have been lost to the ravages of time but would still, today, in just the memory of them, inspire artists across the world. Had there been kings, she would've been the very first.

A girl like that is not easily impressed. So the youth appealed to the gods. Three of the gods heard and were generous.

The first god gave the youth a net, with which he could catch fish, and a knife, or something like a knife, with which he could clean his catch. And this youth was first of all mankind to catch a fish, prepare a fish – with some salt and pepper – and serve fish grilled. He fed the village, if it could be called a village at so early a time in history.

The girl ate the fish, and liked the fish, and thanked the youth. But nothing changed.

The second god gave the youth a sack of seeds, which he planted in a field, the first seeds ever to be planted in all of time. Plants burst forth, first as stems and vines and bushes, until overnight they blossomed in every color imaginable, and many colors that, while we take them for granted today, had never before existed.

The girl ran through the fields of flowers with all the other girls, the children, and the animals. They made garlands and necklaces and filled stone vases. But by the time the blooms faded, nothing had changed.

The third god gave the youth fermented grapes, from which he made the first wine. Like everything else, he gave this to everyone, and though it was deliriously delicious, still nothing changed.

Despite the three gifts of the gods, the youth had failed to win his love. He wandered hopelessly through the woods until he came upon a river, and there he sat on a boulder and wept. They were brilliantly intense, those tears, and the skies cried in sympathy.

After some time, he looked up and saw the girl. She had come after him into the woods. She was smiling.

"You brought me dinner, and that was nice," she said, in the language of their time so the translation is approximate. "You gave the whole world flowers, and I know that you gave them to me. You brought us wine, and I don't think we'll ever celebrate anything quite the same as we did before. Did you think I wanted these things?"

"I don't know that I was thinking at all."

"You weren't," she agreed. "And you aren't now. I appreciate those things, but they are not what I want."

"You want my heart," he said.

Her smile grew larger then. "I want your heart."

"It's yours," he said.

But the girl shook her head. "It's not so easy. Convince me. Tell me. Use every word you can imagine, and make up new ones, but to show how much you love me."

And that is how poetry was created.

9 JANUARY

She gathered all the things she thought might be necessary: an assortment of spices, a candle and matches, dried rose petals, wine, a bottle of ink and the right pen, a small silver mirror, a tiny bell, two Russian thimbles, and a photograph of her grandfather.

She didn't actually need any of those things, but she clung to ceremony. She lit the candle, she spread the spices and the rose petals, she even served herself tea. She filled the thimbles with wine and rang the bell and said a few ancient words in the proper order. Then she waited. She was prepared to wait a long time, and he made her wait a very long time indeed, past midnight, until the clock chimed three the next morning.

The third chime hadn't finished its echo when he bent down, picked up one of the thimbles, and drank the offering. "Hello, my little Mouse."

He looked nothing like the young man in the black and white photo, but he still looked strong and solid.

"Grandpa," she said, drinking her thimbleful.

"You're getting to be quite the talent," he told her.

"I've been sitting here three hours," she said.

"I had a long way to go." He sat in his favorite rocking chair, which of course was still in the living room. It creaked gently.

"I've been studying," she said.

"I know."

"I brought the rain."

"I'm proud of you, Mouse."

"And I've met a man."

"Do you love him?"

"No."

"But he's good to you?"

"He is."

"And you want my help?"

She got suddenly shy. She looked away, lowered her voice. "You promised you'd come and help when the time came."

"I expected something different, my little Mouse, but of course I will help you."

"Thank you."

So her grandfather told her the things she needed, the precise measurements, the order of inclusion, the method of consumption. "Best in a hot drink," he said, "but not tea. Chocolate."

"I can do that, Grandpa."

"Of course you can. I taught you well."

They got up and hugged goodbye. Her grandfather stepped sideways, out of sight, to begin his journey back to the place from which he came.

She realized, then, her mistake. In Seattle, she was three hours ahead of her grandfather's Florida home. He had made the journey at precisely midnight, his time.

The next night, she prepared a special dinner for the man she'd met. He was gentle and courteous and complimentary. He was smooth and cool and he did all the right things. At the meal's end, she broke out the homemade hot chocolate, two steaming mugs of it.

They shared it by the fireplace, the crackling of the fire the only sound. She waited for the chocolate to have its effect.

They both became sleepy. She suggested they sleep there, in front of the fire, warm and close together. By midnight, they both slept soundly, and the fire died down.

She woke at dawn, still in his arms. The potion had worked. She was in love.

10 JANUARY

When the night is darkest and coldest, long after midnight but far from dawn, when even the cat's asleep, they arrive. There are nine this night – perhaps more or less on another. They enter through a hole in the wall, like mice, or a break in reality, each from another direction, each reaching the bed in their own way. They pull themselves up the sheets hanging over the edge. They scale the legs of the bed. They drop down from the dresser or the ceiling fan. They surround the sleeping girl, then crawl closer, across her ankles, over her stomach, up her forearm. One climbs onto her face and feels the gentle rhythm of her breathing. And one by one, they slip under her skin and into her consciousness. They are Mares, the wranglers of nightmares, and why should tonight be any different from any other night?

Abruptly, her breathing changes. Her eyes snap open, catching, in the murk, one quarter-foot tall Mare standing on the bit of skin between her upper lip and her nose.

It's barely 3am. The nightmares had already started. She's not really awake, not really asleep. And the Mare, so unused to being caught in the act, freezes.

She opens her mouth, perhaps to yawn; but like a cat, she snatches the Mare in her maw and swallows him whole.

She coughs and gags, but it's too late. She sits up, suddenly quite awake, trying to dislodge the wriggling thing in her throat.

The other Mares, eight of them, find themselves quite forcibly ejected.

The Mares try to scatter, but she's too fast for them, still embodied with a bit of dreamland strength and agility. She catches them all and puts them in a shoebox. They yell at her, they curse her, they shake their tiny little fists.

She shakes her head. "No more," she says. She closes the shoebox and puts a heavy book on top so they can't get out.

She gets a glass of water in the bathroom to better wash down the Mare she's swallowed. Then she goes back to sleep.

It's blissful, uninterrupted, without night terrors or dark landscapes or wicked dreams. When she wakes, her tummy is a little upset, but it's not too bad. She checks on her captives in the shoebox. Since the sun has risen, they've gone dormant, and they can barely protest.

She says, "Sleep, little ones."

Over the next few days, she feeds them bacon strips and lettuce leaf and a saucer of milk, which the cat finds disconcerting. When she walks down the streets, she sees the shapes of strangers' fears. Spiders here, public speaking, falling, rejection, clowns. In a bar, she touches a man's arm as he flirts with her, and she sees the walls closing around him, the swell of darkness, the crush of a constricting ceiling. He runs outside, seeking space and air. She laughs, but not too loudly. At night,

she sleeps deeply, though the sun seems to tire her and the moon mourns the hours without her.

The fifth night, before midnight, she opens the shoebox and looks down at her captives. She says, "I'm hungry." She catches one by his leg and pops him, without salt, down her throat. A little bit of whiskey helps him go down more smoothly.

She goes out, and now doesn't even need to touch her victim. A random young girl breaks into a fit of screaming that ends with hyperventilating and tranquilizers.

The next night, she opens the shoebox on seven Mares and licks her lips. She takes two, one after the other. The family down the hall all wake up simultaneously and flee a burning building that never burned.

The next night, she eats three. They're harder to swallow in such a quantity, but she's gotten used to the taste. They're quite potent, flavorful and thoroughly frightening. In the city, she doesn't just create vivid, overwhelming nightmares for the sleeping and the wakeful, she gives them form and substance. Knife-wielding clowns run rampant in the streets, some riding on the backs of reptilian raptors.

The next night, only three Mares remain. She dips them in chocolate. After, she thinks she should have thought of that sooner.

The night is young. No one sleeps. The world suffers universal night tremors that incapacitate nations and industry. Lovers quarrel. Trains stop running. There's a suicide.

That catches her attention, as it was never part of her plan. To tell the truth, she never had a plan, never meant to swallow the first Mare, but they were like candy. Like drugs. Like ice cream. She couldn't stop.

Days pass. No one sleeps. Circles under sunken eyes become prevalent, then unavoidable. She, and she alone – perhaps her cat – can sleep through the day. Things stalk the shadows, things she never imagined, the distorted nightmares of seven billion sleepless zombies.

For her, it's a living nightmare, and she knows it's nothing next to what others suffer, but she has no control. It broadcasts from her and through her, nightmares made real, ultra-real, and supra-real. She takes to screaming and pulling out her hair in clumps.

Everyone else knows it's her. They watch her, stare at her, follow her, and stalk her. They gape from the windows and doorways and alleys, moaning, pleading, crying, begging. She runs, but they're everywhere. They point at her with blood-stained fingers. They scream. They cackle. They gather outside her apartment door, on the fire escapes, on the rooftops across the street. She can't get away from them. They don't let her sleep.

She breaks and screams and bolts upright in bed, spitting out the first Mare.

The others escape, racing across her sheets, off the bed, evading the cat and vanishing uncaught. But one, wet with her spit, straightens himself and looks at her and grins.

"That," she says, panting and sweating, her heart racing, "was uncalled for."

He bows and says, "And now that I've seen your heart, oh would-be Queen of Nightmares, I can only promise worse."

She swats at him, meaning to crush him like a bug, but by the time her hand crashes on the bed he's stepped sideways and disappeared.

For the rest of that night, until dawn breaks, the cat tries to comfort her. It does no good. She drinks a glass of water and wonders how long she can keep awake before going insane.

11 JANUARY

The city was old and gray. It's never quiet, it's never dull, it's full of color in all the secret corners and hide-aways and personal spaces.

Outside, there were bridges stretching to other shores, and cars that would take you far away, but the streets almost all ended within the confines of the city and the subways wouldn't take you out of it. They went around and around underground, stopping at the same platforms every time – every time, that was, except this once.

This one time, the subway stopped at a desolate, abandoned platform, which it often passed, and one boy, Bobby, stuck his head out the doors, looked up and down, and stepped off the train.

The concrete here was old. It crumbled in places. Faded paint peeled off the walls. There were advertisements, jeans and perfume and opera, but they were older than Bobby.

The train doors closed and left him alone.

The lights at the station shone dim, but glowed nonetheless, which had to mean something. Someone paid to keep the lights on.

Bobby admitted his worldview was skewed. Trains did exist that took you north of the city or west, or even south, should you feel a need for self-inflicted punishment. But no trains stopped here. The tiles on the wall called it *Rue de L'illusion*, which was the wrong language but easy to translate.

"Hello!" he called out. His voice ran down long halls, turning here and there, eventually returning with no real answer. Bobby left the platform in the most logical direction, passing deep shadows and closed-up newsstands, until he reached a set of stairs rising to daylight.

He climbed.

Bobby thought he knew his home city. He had been to all the edges. He had visited museums and bookshops and candy stores. He had seen the very rich with their fancy cars and well-dressed doormen, and he had seen the very poor with their tattered dreams and scraps of hope. He had seen crime and passion and business and beggars. He had seen bankers and bakers and lawyers – and even the mayor. He had, in his fourteen years, explored every road, street, avenue, lane, and alley. He had seen rooftop gardens and dirt lots no more than ten feet wide. But these particular streets were new to him, never before seen, occupied by buildings that weren't near as gray as the rest of his city. And the streets were quiet, empty and abandoned. He walked in the middle of the street, arms outstretched, a thing that would get him killed in any other part of the city.

He walked for a while, and everything was new but dirty, promising but silent.

Eventually, he discovered he was not alone. A girl stood in the street. She wore a faded dress and had blonde hair. She stared at him.

"Hi," he said.

"Hi."

"I'm Bobby. What's your name?"

"I don't have a name yet."

"How can you not have a name yet? What does that mean? When do you get a name?"

"When you name me."

"That's silly," Bobby said. He was often honest and free-spoken. "You just don't want to tell me. Fine. I don't care."

She frowned.

He said, "Name yourself."

"I always like Jenny."

"There you go," Bobby said. "You have a name after all."

She smiled.

"Where is everyone?" he asked.

"There isn't anyone."

"This is a city," he said. "There's always someone." He glanced toward the highest buildings, but recognized nothing in the skyline. He looked all around in every direction.

"You haven't given the city anyone yet," Jenny said.

He laughed. "You're weird. I like you."

"I like you too."

They stood there, in the middle of the street, between unfamiliar towers of concrete and steel, staring awkwardly at each other.

Finally, Bobby asked, "How do I get home?"

"Go back the way you came."

"I'm in a fairy world, aren't I?" Bobby asked. He'd always had something of an imagination.

"Not exactly."

The sun was dipping in the sky. He really should go home. It felt unnatural, this vacant section of city.

"I'll be here again tomorrow," she told him.

Bobby went back the way he came. The station remained empty. The turnstiles accepted his token. He reached the empty platform, and soon a subway stopped and its doors opened for him.

After climbing aboard, after the doors slid shut, he looked out at the platform and saw Jenny standing there looking sad. She turned her head to watch him leave but did not wave.

The next day, the subway did not stop at the abandoned platform. They passed it so quickly, you couldn't even read its name in the tiled wall.

Bobby asked about the abandoned station, but no one knew anything – not the conductor, not the cop, not the guy selling the dailies and bottled water. He went to the library but found nothing. The librarian even went so far as to tell him there were no abandoned subway stations; although old maps might show some, she said they were traps in the maps, not real, meant to deter map thieves.

Bobby didn't know if he believed in map thieves until he become one himself, slipping an old subway schedule into his back pocket before leaving the library.

The librarian gave him a funny look but didn't stop him.

A year passed, but Bobby was never able to convince the subway to stop at a station no one believed existed. He stopped trying. He took to books instead, and sketching the girl's face with pencils. He started writing poetry for her, and stories about all the hidden, magical corners of cities. He wrote about tiger trainers and actors and old men making chocolate. He sketched the faces of the hidden city's policemen, mobsters, bankers, and politicians. He wrote a great many stories, few of them any good. And one day, after another year had passed, sixteen year old Bobby was surprised when the subway stopped at *Rue de L'illusion.*

This time, the platform was not empty, though no one got on the subway and only Bobby got off.

Jenny was there. She wore a yellow sundress now. She smiled and took Bobby by the hand and led him to the streets.

"You should give us taxi drivers," she told him. "And janitors. And I'd like to eat something other than chocolate, you know."

"I can't do that," he told her. But he carried his journals and sketchpads in a backpack.

"No one else can," she told him.

So she sent him home, this time with a kiss on the cheek. She said, "I'll be here again tomorrow."

On the train, before it had even left the station, Bobby started writing a story about Jenny. For next time.

12 JANUARY

There's nothing in the attic.

She moved in three weeks ago. She sleeps fine. There are no strange noises, but there is one door she never considered. In the ceiling.

It haunts her now. When she walks through the short hall, to bedroom or bathroom or living room, she doesn't always glance up but she feels the weight of it. The not knowing. The uncertainty. The possibilities.

There might be an antique she could pawn, some rare Russian thimble or a Civil War era rifle or an ivory-handled mirror. There might be evidence of a crime, the secret books with details of shady deals, a murder weapon, a body in a plastic bag stuffed into a trunk.

She has friends over one night for beer and wine and food and music. Sometime near midnight, she tells them about the unopened attic like it's a ghost story. What if simply opening the attic door unleashes some demonic entity bent on possession and sex and death? What if she finds that tattered, dusty remnants of a jilted bride's gown and the bride didn't want to be disturbed? What if a spring-loaded, rust-coated trap is set to spring?

No one opens the attic door that night.

She doesn't have a step ladder. Eventually, after a few weeks fending off questions about spiders, squirrels, skeletons, and lost silverware, she drags a chair beneath the attic entrance. It's merely a thin piece of wood. She pushes it up and out of the way. The attic is dark, and high above her. The chair is barely enough for her to drag herself up.

She retrieves a flashlight first. With a little bit of struggle, she hauls herself into the low, slope-ceiling attic.

It's not really much more than a crawl space. She shines the light into the corners, disturbing dry cobwebs, leaving eddies of shadow in the beam's wake. There's no floor, only the narrow edge of 2x4s crisscrossing a sea of pink insulation. There are no mice, no chests, no forgotten artwork, nothing by way of treasure. There's one discarded tee shirt, small enough for a child, too small for her. It's red, but the graphic on its front is cracked, faded, and indecipherable.

Partly out of respect, partly cleanliness, and yes, partly for fear, she takes the tee shirt with her when she leaves. She climbs down without incident. The chair holds her. She doesn't fall. She closes up the attic and, as there's no reason not to, she forgets about it.

And why not? There's nothing in the attic.

But she had a dream once, as a child, that she visited her godmother's apartment in New York. In reality, past the front door there had been a kitchen on the left, doors to a bathroom and a bedroom on the right. But in the dream, another door had been squeezed between them, opening onto a staircase climbing to an attic that had never existed in New York City. Maybe twelve at the time, she'd ascended into darkness and discovered an extra, hidden room, with a window overlooking the greenest garden that never existed and a very old roll top desk. Every time she visited her godmother after that, despite that there were apartments on the floor above, and more apartments above that, she would check, just to make sure, that another unseen door didn't simply appear. It never did.

That extra door decided to make its real life appearance in her rented house a week after she explored the empty attic.

The extra door had appeared between her bedroom and the bathroom. She knew there would be stairs. She knew the house had a second, hidden attic, and it would not be empty.

Once she saw it, she couldn't look away, not to get her phone to call someone, not to retrieve that flashlight, not to put on proper clothes. A door like this only gave you one chance to open it.

Finally, she grabbed the knob. It turned easily. She knew there wouldn't be a lock. On the other side: stairs led up into darkness.

She ascended.

She left the door open behind her, though she doubted it would matter.

At the top of the stairs she had to turn to see the hidden attic. The top was lowered on the roll top desk. The window looked out onto some other-worldly garden.

There was only enough light to see by. She went to the desk and opened it. She found papers, a fancy fountain pen, a letter opener, several old photographs of people she almost recognized.

"Cassandra."

At the sound of her name, she turned around. Her godmother stood at the top of the stairs, looking just as she had all those years ago in New York.

"My, you've grown."

"Am I dreaming?" Cassandra asked.

"You are," her godmother said. "But you're also awake."

"I've seen this room before."

"I know. I've done a lot of writing at that desk. I've spent a lot of time staring out that window. But it's not my room anymore, Cassandra. It's my gift to you."

"I should've stayed in touch better. I can call you today."

"You can't. But I'm here now, Cassandra."

"For the last time?"

Her godmother smiled sadly. "Yes."

She looked at the desk, the window, the garden, then back at her godmother, who was no longer there.

She stayed in the room a long time. There were old letters to read, journal entries from her godmother telling amazing stories about unbelievable things that were, in fact, quite believable now.

She didn't want to leave.

But she did. She still had classes, and friends, and real world things to do. But anytime she wanted it, Cassandra needed only look properly at the space between two doors to find her private door and her hidden attic.

13 JANUARY

The city is a stark vertical landscape filled with rough textures, sharp contrasts, grit and shadow, and the ever present sense of mystery, magic, romance, and passion. And the rain on the city: nails dropping from an amorphous steely cloud, accentuating the city's height.

Atop one of the anonymous tall buildings, two warriors face each other, heedless of the elements, weapons ready – sticks for one, long thin rods expertly balanced and just flexible enough; a katana for the other, a heralded blade three centuries old, sharp enough to slice the raindrops in half.

They are both well-trained, experienced, strong, fast, agile, smart, the best of their kind. In their minds, they already know how the fight will go. Through neither has moved, they have already fought. They know every strike, every parry, every evasion. They are intimately familiar with the strengths and weaknesses of their adversary – and of themselves. Neither weapon can be said to be better, nor either warrior. No factor remains unaccounted for – the shadows, the roof's surface, the weather, the cacophonous city sounds rising around them, the struggles each overcame to reach this place at this time.

They are not unseen. At least three recording devices, from different sources, will capture their battle. A half dozen faces hide behind curtains in windows across the alley. Two men, a mile away in different directions, point telescopes at the rooftop. There's a helicopter not far off. And sinister, mystical things have been aroused, creatures of darkness and of light, gambling on the outcome – the stakes beyond the ability of mortals to pay.

The rhythm of the city pulsates on the rooftop, the sounds of traffic and sirens and a hundred thousand televisions, stereos, the feet of dancers on a stage, the rumble of trains on their subterranean tracks. There is, perhaps, time for a breath, a complete inhalation and exhalation, before it begins. The warriors will clash until death ends it.

In that heartbeat of time, a great many things happen across the city: a boy steals his first kiss, a baby comes screaming into the world, a chef serves the last meal of a prisoner condemned, a fashion designer climbs into a yellow taxi, lies are told, truths revealed, an old man alone in apartment exhales his last air. It all combines with the lifebeat of the city, that rhythm, which even now fuels the hearts of two warriors on a rooftop.

There's no bell to signal the start, no whistle or gunshot or flag waved or handkerchief dropped, yet the warriors move at precisely the same moment. They know every curve of the battle, every breath of it, beginning and end. For a thousand watching, the tension is intense, but the warriors are completely at ease, relaxed, loose, and ready. Nothing can distract them from their individual, identical intentions.

That first sound of their weapons connecting is like thunder. The city rocks with it – and realms beyond, where the betting is closed and everyone, creatures of both light and dark, are about to lose. They've come close to see this final round. They've followed the exploits of each warrior on their various years-long quests. Some, in fact, have interfered; the warriors bear scars as proof.

The first sound of their weapons clashing resonates long and deep, the echoes causing every other city sound to recede, the rain to pause, the cameras to flicker, the windows to crackle like spider webs.

That first clash of their weapons shatters, albeit it briefly, the glass veil that separates this mortal city from those unmortal things. It's only a flash, less than a heartbeat – less than a breath – less even than the crack of lightning that explodes in sympathy.

The warriors slip off the rooftop, out of the rain, and into another realm. The greedy bored things that had watched most closely, surprised and overwhelmed and woefully unprepared. The manipulative little shits screech inhumanly as immortality is stolen from them by the impossible weapons of two impossible warriors meant – *destined* – to destroy each other.

The warriors don't get a lot of time in the other world before their own pulls them back, but they do a lot of damage, they spill a lot of blood, they send a powerful message: *Do not meddle in mortal affairs.* The humans may be made of weak flesh and brittle bone, but they can be devious and dangerous and deadly, even facing things that cannot die. Do not meddle in mortal affairs, or risk the truth of your own mortality.

In higher realms still, things even greater notice – and smile.

14 JANUARY

The fog came in ahead of the morning sun, just as the prophecy foretold, but only a handful of people knew about such future prospecting. The strong, solid, most likely scenarios were always kept locked away in underground bunkers, hidden libraries, or terribly well-guarded fortresses. But Mr. Jones understood immediately. He had been waiting, counting down the days, anxious and excited and even a little bit giddy. He had read the signs, such that they were, and he had seen one of the old books.

It was gone now, behind lock and key, safe from public awareness, but Mr. Jones wasn't interested in saving the world.

He got into his off-road, high-tech Land Rover, a beauteous and luxurious vehicle he'd acquired in preparation for this day. The roads were still only lightly used. The way was clear. He drove carefully, not hitting other drivers, some of whom must surely have read the same omens. There had been a gathering of crows the night before, floods in three corners of the map, snow in the north, other signs more disturbing. He obeyed every rule of traffic, the lights and speed limits, yielding rights of way, signaling before every lane shift.

He left the radio off and drove in silence. A copy of *Rolling Stone* lay in the passenger seat. A bottle of water trembled in the console between.

Finally, at the appointed place, Mr. Jones pulled off the road. Yes, he was a little early, but still surprised to find himself alone. There had been indications. Anyone could have seen them.

He didn't much like the idea of being alone, but he was resigned to it.

Mr. Jones switched off the engine to conserve fuel. He rolled down the window. A light, moist breeze drifted across the lot. It amazed him, that he was alone here to be part of this, that he may in fact play a role. But there were other places, surely, like this one, where the same sacrifice might be made.

He glanced often at his watch, but time became putty. He got hungry, but ignored it. He opened the bottle of water, though he knew he should have saved it. Eventually, the time drew nearer. With fifteen minutes remaining, Mr. Jones climbed out of the Land Rover, locked it, armed the alarm, and began the final leg of his journey, the last steps.

He waited at the entryway until some random teenager with keys showed up and let him in.

There was no display. Release day, yet they were relegated to a stack of other new releases, one boy band among rock legends, jazz sirens, pop beauties, and movie soundtracks. Five interchangeable kids stared at him from the front of the CD. He took it to the front counter.

The girl there frowned when she saw what he'd taken to her. Her nametag said Kerri.

"Are you sure?" Kerri asked.

"Someone's got to," Mr. Jones told her. He paid with cash. He said he didn't need a bag. He carried the disc to his Land Rover, unwrapped it in the front seat, and popped it in.

At first, there was silence. Then the first note exploded from the speakers. Then the world blew up, and all life on the planet was lost.

15 JANUARY

To the very edge of the ocean, the forest burns. To the place where the trees reach the beach, where the sky touches the earth, where the water endlessly, ceaselessly, erodes the land. The smoke is thick, struck through with eddies of barely breathable air, but even that is hot and stark and tainted. The fire crackles and cackles, screams and roars, rages with uncontained fury. It consumes the leaves and the trunks and the bushes and the underbrush.

From the very edge of the forest, a girl escapes, coughing and choking. Two, three steps onto the sand, and she stumbles. She falters. She falls.

On the ground, panting, heaving, coated by soot and ash, still she claws at the sand. She pulls herself toward the ocean.

Her clothes were white, if ochre now, her flesh pale, her hair a deep brown and her eyes a brilliant green. She's in tatters, barely alive; she's run a long way. She's tired. But she'd not defeated.

Fire reaches the edge of the forest and scorches the sand, but advances no further. In the flames, a woman stands, her hair red and her eyes red, her white clothes much like her sister's. She stands at the edge of the tree line. She, too, has been running a long way.

The girl in the sand looks back and smiles.

"I hate that smile," her red sister says.

"You've never been fast enough to catch me."

"I came close."

"No, actually, you didn't."

In this place where fire burns through the forest, where sky and ocean touch the shore, two of their other sisters approach, each wearing white, or variations therefore, one with pearl eyes and flowing blonde hair, the other's eyes like the sun and hair very nearly blue.

Always, the four of them, chasing and teasing each other, passing threats but also gifts.

"We're not alone."

"We were never alone."

"There are other powers."

"The humans?" Red asks, still standing in the flames. "I can destroy them all."

"As can I."

"They brought with them four horsemen."

"Only four?"

"Powers."

"Powers that will, in the end, lead to their own destruction."

"There can't be only four."

"There are only four of us," Red says.

"You know that's not true."

'We're the only four that matter."

"But I've seen the horsemen. They can go nowhere without my knowing, and I tell you, they are five."

"And there are other Powers."

"You're not listening to me."

'Four, five, what difference does it make?"

"Oh, the four are terrible, each alone and certainly together, but the fifth horseman – he's something extraordinary."

"We'll outlast them all. We always do."

"Do they have names?"

"Do we?"

They laugh, a sisterly conspiracy. Against the horizon, the setting sun paints the sky in all their colors.

"The fifth horseman is dangerous. I fear him."

"I don't," Red says.

"You don't know Fear."

"Not true. We drink together."

"They bring more than just the horsemen. They bring Muses. Fates. Godlings and shadows and demons."

'I've seen the demons."

'You've seen the demons of the land," says the pearl-eyed sister. "You should see what lurks in the deep. The size of them."

Then Red asks a question that leads to a length of silence. "Have they brought Death?" When she is certain no one wants to answer, Red answers for them: "They have, haven't they?"

"Well, there's the horseman."

"They do have names."

"And is one of them...?"

"Yes," she says. "Yes, damn it all, yes."

"Don't forget the fifth."

"Quiet, girl. We have bigger concerns."

"Death cannot touch us."

"Yet you tremble."

"So do you."

"I don't deny it."

"Should we do anything this time?"

"Why?"

"We could – I don't know, teach them, maybe?"

"It's already too late. They've brought these things into existence, and as always, these things will die with them."

"You're heartless."

"So are you."

"I might take one as a lover."

"I might seek their Death."

"Nonsense. Death can't touch any of us, least of all you."

"I just realized. You're afraid."

"I admit it. They brought that, too."

"What else?"

"What else is there?"

"Love. Hope. Courage."

"Yes, of course, all those things and more. Every time. Why would it be different now?"

"The fifth horseman."

That exasperates all of the sisters. Their conversations are always short. They say their goodbyes and exchange hugs and promises, but the truth is they can hardly stand each other. Family holds them together, and love, and even trust, but each has her own life to live.

The Seasons slip over each other as time passes – another four sisters, though they are closer and only rarely interact with their older sisters.

The girl with the brown eyes walks through her forests, far from the waters, high in the mountains and across plains until she reaches a certain rock.

There, she feels closest to her mother, though in fact she can be no closer than she ever is. She sits against the rock and says, though there's no one there to speak to, "I love you, mother, but I am afraid."

Her mother doesn't answer; but if she did, it would be to say, "You should be."

As the sisters sits, she closes her eyes. Sleep comes swiftly, and with it dreams. She rarely dreams. She hasn't in an age. In the dreamscape, she strolls through gray canyons of glass and brick, where the humans have – or will – congregated. Packed together so tightly, they are easy picking for the horsemen, who ride unseen among them, strikingly randomly and wantonly.

There's Disease, and its affects are bad. There's Famine, and it spreads itself widely across the earth. There's War, bigger and bigger with every passing millennia. There's Death, ever present, ever grinning, who will live only for as long as they are humans.

The Fifth Horseman rides alongside her as she watches the human scenes moving past at unnatural speeds, to kill and suffer and die. It makes her weak. Indeed, as the humans grow stronger, she and her sisters will suffer.

"We don't suffer," she says to the Fifth Horseman.

"That's an old way of thinking," he tells her.

"You're a new one," she says.

"I'm with you now."

"You're a Nightmare."

"So I am."

"Therefore, none of this is real," she says. "It's a manifestation of my fears."

"I'm worse than that," he tells her.

"How so?"

"I facilitate the creation of your fears. Everyone's fears. It's not enough that you dream them. They must be made real to have any power."

"You are a Power."

He grins. "One of the great ones."

She wakes with a start. Much time has passed, not just nights or months or years. The things in her nightmare, they are already beginning to be real.

In the end, the humans will destroy her mother, her sisters, and her. There's no escaping it, unless maybe she and her kin, the elements, can turn their hearts against humankind.

But she cannot find her sisters.

16 JANUARY

The letter arrived without a return address and without a postmark, though it did have Air Mail stamped prominently on it. Don took his time opening it. There were other things in the mail – a book he'd ordered, the phone bill – and he didn't think he knew anyone overseas. He felt no real urge to tear into the letter, but shortly after dinner he got around to reading it.

Donny,

Your presence is requested. Please don't respond by post, but in person.

It was written in a neat, looping style, feminine though he couldn't be sure. An airline ticket was enclosed, and several few hundred dollars – almost a week's pay. It wasn't a lot of money, but the destination, Paris, was far away and a place he'd never been.

He didn't simply take time off from work and go. First, he verified that the ticket was real; it was, though the airline refused to say who had paid for it. He checked the money, too, with one of those anti-counterfeit pens from the office supply store.

Whoever had written the letter had him intrigued. He got the time off, fished out his passport from its barely-seen hiding place, and crossed the Atlantic.

He didn't know what to do or where to go when he landed at Charles de Gaulle, but he didn't have to worry. A chauffer in a crisp suit and sunglasses carried a placard with his name on it.

The chauffer either didn't speak English or pretended not to, and Don's knowledge of French language didn't go far past *croissant*. They drove mostly in silence, Don in the backseat watching the scenery.

After a while, they reached the city, which was bigger than Don expected, but just as French. He saw many postcard-ready side streets but nothing he recognized – no tower, no church – before stopping in front of a rather regular looking building.

A woman greeted Don at the door. She was dressed very businesslike and wore her hair in a tight bun, but she was young and spoke English smoothly, albeit with a gorgeous accent. "Jean will handle your bags, if you'd like to come with me."

"Did you send me the letter?" he asked.

"No." She held open the door for him. "If you please."

Don entered the lobby, in which there were couches, a rack of pamphlets and maps, and a counter. The girl at the counter didn't look up, and Don's guide walked right by her.

"In Paris," she said, "we have the best food in the world, and you have dinner reservations already made, but you didn't come all this way for escargot, did you?"

"Actually," Don admitted, "I'm not sure why I came all this way."

In a tiny alcove, there was a single elevator door. They got on and went down to the basement, to a long hall with insufficient lights, but Don's guide seemed not to notice. They passed several opens doors revealing laundry facilities, storage, and canned goods, as well as several closed doors. At one of these, she took a key from her pocket, pulled the door open, and motioned Don inside.

She didn't follow. Rather, she shut and locked the door, leaving Don in a conference room. A dozen chairs surrounded the table, but only one was occupied.

The woman there was older, matronly, with something of a scowl permanently etched onto her features. She got to her feet and tried to smile. "Sit."

Don sat. He purposefully passed the nearest chair, but didn't quite travel half the table's length.

"Thank you for coming on such short notice."

Don didn't respond, but she seemed to wait for him to do so. He said, "Thank you."

She shook her head. "You won't be thanking me when we are done. Call me Isador."

"Is that not your name?" Don asked.

"No."

He shrugged. "Okay, then, Isador. You got me here. What for?"

She tried to smile again. Someone should tell her not to bother. She said, "You're the last descendant, since my husband died. It's all yours."

"I don't know what you mean."

"My daughter – you've already met her, Jolene – she is my daughter, not his. I have no other children. He had no other, except one."

"Not me."

"No. Your mother."

Don didn't know what to say, so he said, "Oh."

"You see what I mean, then?"

"I think so."

"It all goes to you, then."

Don't stomach twisted. He wasn't sure of what to expect, though of course he'd always wished for a rich uncle. "What goes to me?"

"The piano. The wine. What's left of the money. The key." This, she placed on the conference table before her, on top of a manila envelope that had already been there. "And of course," she added, pushing her chair back and standing again, "what it unlocks."

She walked around the table, away from Don, and went to the door, where she paused. "Take your time," she said, knocking twice on the door. It opened immediately. "Jolene will be here when you're ready. You'll be wanting to sample our dining."

They locked Don in, alone with an envelope and a key.

He waited a respectable amount of time before going to the end of the table and opening the envelope. The papers inside included a picture of a two hundred year old piano and details about its heritage; a listing of forty-two bottles of wine; and financial papers indicating a balance of almost five thousand Euros – which was not a substantial sum. He saw where his airline ticket and cash had been withdrawn, and a room paid for, presumably upstairs from here.

That left only the key, for which there was no paperwork, no deed, no indication of what it unlocked. It was old and heavy, not like any key Don has ever used. He returned all the papers to the envelope and pocketed the key.

When he knocked on the door, there was a brief delay before Jolene opened it. Isador, whoever she was, had gone.

"Dinner?" Jolene asked.

"What does the key open?" he asked.

"Trust me," she said, "you'll want to eat first."

They left the hotel and walked to a cozy little restaurant where the staff ignored him and conversed only with Jolene, but the food was incredibly delicious, the best Don had ever had. The sauce was impossible, the wine a perfect compliment.

He tried several times to learn either the name of his grandfather or the purpose of the key, but Jolene kept the conversation light and utterly meaningless. She paid with a card. He wondered, albeit briefly, if she'd used his money.

"Now," Jolene said, standing, "shall we reveal your kingdom?"

They took a taxi to a grungy part of the city, where the shops had already closed and were protected by cages and gates, where the graffiti was crude and rarely artistic. The streets were mostly barren and mostly dark, and the streetlights virtually useless.

They stopped at a doorway tucked quietly between two shops that weren't closed just for the night. The paint was peeling off the door and the jamb, but it looked solid and heavy. An old padlock held it shut.

Don didn't need any prompting. He took a deep breath of air, uncertain if the quality inside would be even worse, and used the key.

He pushed the door open onto a dark, narrow set of stairs. Jolene came up behind him. At the top, to one side, there was another door, this one unlocked.

He fumbled for a light switch but didn't find it. Jolene stepped in behind him and flipped the switch. A single bare bulb struggled to bring shadows into the room. It failed to provide much by way of light; it just made the gloom easier to see.

The gloom – and the dolls. Dozens. No – hundreds, with porcelain faces and glass eyes and dresses from which all the color had drained. Don scanned the room, seeing nothing else. The dolls sat on shelves and on tables and on the floor. Many were stacked tightly against each other, while others seemed to have been given more space. Many had human hair, or something near enough.

They stared vacantly, all of them, at Don and the door. They were quiet. Unnaturally still. The shadows blanketed them. There was a window, but it had been blacked out.

Don stared for a long time, though he didn't move. Jolene, beside him, said nothing. In the harsh absence of light, the dolls seemed to be in a constant state of motion just outside his peripheral vision.

Some were newer than others. A few seemed incredibly old. Some stood stiffly against the wall. Others sat quietly. Some had fallen over or flopped to one side.

"My grandfather was a doll maker," Don said.

"From a long line of doll makers," Jolene told him.

"You couldn't tell me this?"

"It seemed important to show you the vastness of your empire."

"It's not much of an empire," Don said.

"No," Jolene admitted. "But it's all yours." She left the room, descended the stairs, not waiting for Don to follow. She went out the door, leaving Don alone in a cramped room stuffed with oddly life-like effigies in a dark, abandoned corner of Paris. He walked through the room, picking up a doll here or there, marveling at the bits that made them appear unreal.

Eventually, he sat in the middle of his empire of dolls and cried. He cried for the grandfather he never knew, for the dreams he'd lost, childhood fantasies, the life he'd wanted and the life he had, and he cried because his grand Parisian inheritance would change none of that.

When he left the room, Jolene was waiting outside with a taxi. She hugged him like a distant cousin. They went back to the hotel. Don carried one of the dolls with him.

17 JANUARY

The spirits drift, mostly without a sound, across fields and between trees and around the corners of the highest mountains. They whisper to each other. They tell stories, and re-tell those stories to strangers, other spirits, higher and lesser creatures, anyone who might listen.

The spirits drift like smoke, shifting and dissipating, ever in a state of transformation.

Sometimes, one of the spirits will take on a more substantial form, often out of boredom or curiosity, sometimes with a mind toward justice, once in an age for beauty.

Such a thing happened, the mist taking flesh, under the light of a crescent moon – a feat of unbelievable strength and will – after sensing a beautiful thing and coming closer to see the young man bathing in the river.

The mist took a feminine shape, although she never completely shed her ethereal aspect. She approached the man at the river.

"I am but a dream," she said to him, which is as truthful as a spirit can be.

"I have had dreams," the man said, emerging from the river, "but I have never seen one such as you." He dried himself and dressed, never taking his eyes from her. "You must be cold," he said.

"I do not feel the cold," the spirit said.

"Are you hungry? Tired? Lost?"

"None of these things."

He smiled and touched her cheek gently. "Ah, but you are not in love. I can see the spirit in you. It is not your way."

"You know the truth of me," the spirit admitted. "I came closer to..."

She didn't finish what she meant to say. The man shushed her and spoke in a whisper. "I know why you're here. To give yourself to me. And I accept."

For the man was a magician, and recognizing the spirit, he bound her to him. "Until death," he said, meaning hers, "or love."

This made her afraid. She protested. "But I can know neither."

"Then you'll be my servant a long, long time."

The magician was something of a wicked man, though he had no grand intentions. He made her steal for him, sometimes gold and sometimes bread. He made her open locks. He made her poison an innkeeper who had tried to cheat him. He made her hide him in shadows when others intended him harm.

He also made her feed a beggar girl. He made her protect a gypsy falsely accused of giving false prophecy. He made her learn to dance. He made her deliver justice upon the head of an unjust judge.

The magician grew old, but the spirit knew nothing of age. He told his stories of heroes and romance and trickery. She gave him stories of ancient feuds and unsolvable puzzles and sharp-tongued fiends.

They travelled frequently, walking from town to town, making friends and enemies, none of which would be for life, never staying much longer than a fortnight.

One foggy evening, between towns, as the rain came down in slow, lazy drops the size of your thumb, they were ambushed by bandits. Almost immediately, one stabbed the spirit in the back. His sword burst out between her breasts. She leaked mist into the fog. The magician, enraged, killed the lot of them, eleven in all, saving the swordsman for last. The things he did to that would-be murderer before he finally died defy description.

The magician did his best to heal the spirit, but she could not be saved. On the ground, in the magician's arms, she shed a single ethereal tear like a diamond and said, "But I cannot die."

"But you are dying," the magician said. He also cried.

She lifted a weak hand to his cheek. "You are not wounded."

"You are," he said. "It is the same."

She smiled and said, "I believe you."

Two impossible things happened that night. The magician, understanding neither, and indeed understanding much less than that, took a room in the next village and locked himself inside it.

For days, the magician never emerged from his room, until finally the innkeeper had the door broken open. The magician was found dead, petrified, a statue of solid mist and diamond tears. His room became a shrine, and the innkeeper a rich man.

18 JANUARY

It was a classic romance, by some definition.

The boy met the girl in their teens. They went out a few times, ran away to different colleges, lost each other's numbers.

Boy became an accountant for criminal enterprises, where, by necessity, he learned various means of self-defense.

Girl became a master chef and opened her own restaurant to rave reviews.

Boy's boss ordered a hit. It went down in the girl's restaurant, and it went ugly. The target got away.

The girl went after the assassin. She was a chef. She had knife skills. The assassin had no chance.

The target turned back and went after the boss. In the showdown, neither survived and much was destroyed.

Boy went out to get drunk and consider his future employment. The girl went out to get drunk and figure some way to re-build her restaurant.

Boy and girl got drunk together. Recognized each other. Explored their individual pasts, the present, the future.

As I said, it was a classic romance, and there should've been nothing to get in their way. He had money. She had skills. They had dreams, big dreams, and their love was real.

Did I mention the time travelling aliens? Popped into our time in the newly opened restaurant. Critics ran screaming. The aliens had ray guns, after all.

But that wasn't enough to get in the way of their love.

Did I mention the radioactive monster tearing up the streets? The National Guard had to take it down.

What about the supernatural circus made up of ghouls, magicians, creeps, freaks, murderers, and pickpockets?

The mad arsonist blowing up everything he could blow up, buildings and limousines and finally himself?

The ghost with her head on backwards?

There was a ninja.

None of these things did any damage to the love shared by the boy and the girl. The trust between them was unshakable. The love unprecedented. They laughed together and cried together and ate the most exquisite meals.

No, the thing that stuck a wedge between them was a photographer with a 600mm telephoto lens.

Is there a moral to this story? Don't get caught. It's not a good moral, but it's honest. How about this, then: don't do something you wouldn't want to see captured in full color and painful detail on the front page of a supermarket tabloid.

19 JANUARY

A light skips across the edge of the woods – a reflection perhaps, nothing grand or bright.

These are no great or fabled wood, not an ancient forest. There are no dark stories or forbidding tales, no suggestion that anything has ever gone awry. And it borders the back of a condominium complex.

Any other day, Martin might not have noticed the light. But tonight, half a bottle of wine deep, sitting on his back porch in the light of a crescent moon, he notices.

There's a small pond behind his condo, woods on one side of it and behind it, a line of condos coming around the other edge. There's nothing magical in a place like this. Every home is like every other, the cars lined up outside nearly carbon copies of each other.

So when Martin sees the light, he reaches no mystical conclusion. He doesn't comment on it; he's drinking alone tonight. He doesn't rise from his chair. He merely watches the light.

It's a small light, but constant, neither fickle nor flickering, and it knows it's been noticed, so the light dances and leaps and skirts dangerously close to the pond's shore.

In another time, at another place, when magic might have been something to believe in – and even something to expect – the light would have played. It might have been called a fairy by someone who didn't know better, a fairy light, an elf light, a will-o-the-wisp. It might have lured Martin into the woods when all woodland was filled with danger and mystery and romance.

Instead, Martin pours himself another glass of wine and dwells on his sorrows, whatever they might be, however unimportant.

Eventually, Martin gathers himself, which is quite a chore, and goes inside. He falls asleep – or passes out – on the couch with the television on.

The light creeps in through a window. It explores the corners and edges of the inside and finds them constrictive. Reaching the living room, the light hovers over Martin as he snores.

The light sighs.

The light fades and leaves.

Martin, at the last moment, opens his eyes. He's almost seen something. He still feels the wine in him, and the sorrows he meant to drown. *Next time*, he tells himself: *whiskey.*

He goes upstairs and sleeps properly, in his bed and under covers.

The light, meanwhile, drifts to a place where condominiums have not yet invaded.

The light is not alone. Creatures of all types gather in groups or wander or simply stare into the sky. Here, the moon is closer, and she is warmer, and she is almost always kind.

The light finds a shadow it recognizes, and together the two lament the loss of humanity in silence.

Martin sleeps dreamlessly and wakes with a hangover, but he doesn't care. He isn't going to do anything, anyhow. He swallows aspirin and a great deal of water and sits outside on his porch. He doesn't touch the wine, but he stares at the pond and the woods.

He stares for a long time, struggling to get his head working. Finally, he says, "I received a visitor last night."

Without a will-o-the-wisp to guide him in his folly, Martin ventures into the woods and is lost.

20 JANUARY

Trumpets sound in the distance, and the hunt is on. Run, little fox, or the dogs will catch you, and the men with their rifles will sight you and shoot you and skin you and eat you.

In many ways, it's the same as it always was, little fox, but clearly the rules have changed. What was once a fair challenge has been overwhelmingly tilted into the favor of the hunters. Where once you might have had thousands and thousands of acres in which to evade the hunters' bullets and knives, now there are fences and dangerous highways and other critters fighting for the same slight refuge.

Run through the woods, little fox, but already the dogs have your scent, and the men on their horses are getting closer. You can smell their rancid stench and hear their excited yells.

There has always been a hunt. Once upon a time, little fox, a man alone would chase your ancestor on foot, armed perhaps with a club or a makeshift blade of questionable durability. A man alone chasing a fox – that was a fair contest, and it didn't always end in bloodshed.

You're a wily one, little fox, though I'm not sure turning back to their cabin will be of much use. There, they have additional implements of killing, all the tools of cooking, and boxes and boxes of ammunition.

There's a gunshot. They've taken a rabbit. I'm sorry, little fox; that might have been your dinner tonight. Yes, there's a moment of celebration amongst the hunters, but don't mistake their brief joy for satisfaction. There are not after rabbit, though it will make a fine stew. The hunt is still on.

Ah, I see you've already got a way inside the cabin, so even if they locked the doors you're safely inside. Look around, little fox. See if there's anything to help you. The dogs are fast on your trail. You haven't got much by way of time.

The hunters circle the cabin in two groups, surrounding it from both directions. I count five of them, little fox, and three dogs – too many to fight on your own.

I wonder: *are* you alone, little fox?

You're desperate. The dogs won't stop barking. Two of the hunters have dismounted and approach the door. What will they do to you, little fox, if they catch you alive? The dogs have found your point of entrance. There's no way out of the cabin.

Obviously, little fox, you are done running, and you've transformed, taking on your feminine aspect, which an age ago might have been a surprise to these hunters but not today.

I admit, little fox, you are a beautiful creature.

They're inside, the two of them, and you're waiting for them gloriously nude and perfectly displayed. Even seasoned hunters such as these can be momentarily distracted by such fine, delicate grace. They don't even see the rifle in your hands – one of their own – until you've pulled the trigger. Crafty little fox. You're quick enough with the second shot, and accurate with both – but the other three, the younger hunters, less experienced but more emotional, come quick behind them with weapons already raised.

The next shot takes out the middle hunter. Sly little fox, you didn't fire it. The front hunter, surprised, turns but never fully realizes what has happened. Your shot is low this time, and you must shoot again rather than mercilessly prolong his agony.

You drop the rifle after that. You run to the last hunter. He opens his arms to catch your embrace. You kiss, the hunter and the little fox in human guise, the forbidden lovers. You shut the door to keep out the dogs. You have fresh rabbit for stew. You have the warmth of his mortal body, nearly as perfect in its masculinity as yours in its femininity. You're both strong, and your lovemaking wild, and you feed your hunter the most incredible of dreams.

In the morning, little fox, you leave him, and in pity you give the dogs the leftover rabbit, and you go back to your own world.

But I know your secret, little fox – your secret hunter lover. I know your passions go deep. I know how it breaks your heart to leave him.

I feel sad for you, little fox, but I will keep your secret. For now.

21 JANUARY

Corvette Stingray.

Let that sink in a moment. You've probably got a pre-conceived notion that looks a lot like mine: a '72 with curves over those front tires, long and sleep, a fast as hell work of art.

For a long time, the Corvette was America's premiere sports car. But there have been several re-designs, economic upheavals, a changing face of corporate America. In 1982, the last Stingray rolled off the assembly line.

Someone should have noticed. Chevy sold 30 or 40 thousand of them every year. It was an icon, a member of the pop culture elite, yet at some point it became merely the de-facto answer to the midlife crisis.

For a brief time, I had the chance to drive a white '95 Corvette. It was, unfortunately, an automatic. But the *power*. Seriously, when the light turns green in a regular car, you let go of the brake and apply some gas to move that car forward. With the Corvette, you're restraining a beast with your foot jammed down on that brake; let up just a little, it will burst forward.

In its heart, the Corvette has always been such a beast. And maybe we didn't notice when they started to tame down its look – maybe a bit more aerodynamic but losing some level of excitement. What was once distinctive became almost mundane. Only 11,647 new Corvettes were brought to the world in 2012. 13,596 in 2011. There hasn't been a major re-design in nine years. The Corvette, sadly, was becoming just another car.

Yes, it's still an icon. It's got 60 years of history. It is still the dream car du jour of many red-blooded Americans. But ask around a bit, and you'll find people looking to the past, to the '63 or the '72, maybe the '58 or the '67. You think of Alan Shepard, whose 'Vette is displayed at the Kennedy Space Center. You think of Price's Red Corvette. You think of Route 66.

The truth is, the Corvette never stopped being America's premiere sports car. It never gave up any of its power or magnificence. However, in popular culture, its excitement has dwindled.

There hasn't been a Stingray since 1982. Not until now.

It's new. It looks like a Corvette should – how the Stingray would have evolved into the 21st Century.

They say it's got 450 horses, that it's the most fuel efficient Corvette ever, that it's given up its fiberglass for composite and carbon-fiber, and its all-new V-8 goes from 0 to 60 in under four seconds. General Motors knows you might not buy it; but they hope you'll come to look at the Corvette and still go home with a new Chevy. Maybe a Malibu.

I don't care about any of that. I want to get behind the wheel of one of these new Stingrays, drop it into gear, and unleash the new beast.

The excitement is back.

22 JANUARY

The old god huddled under his blanket, crouched in the middle of the living room, shivering, cursing in forgotten languages. He hadn't paid the electric bill again. He also hadn't eaten anything but a raw, scrawny rat he'd managed to catch – what, three days ago?

It was a blizzard out there, the likes of which were unheard of in his old country. There, it had been glory and warmth year round, and his people had marched far in every direction to conquer in his name. There'd been women, endless feasts, music – he missed the music most.

Another night, he might've escaped his misery by finding a band at any bar or club. It didn't matter if they worshipped blues, soul, country, or rap, so long as they were loud and earnest. But this night, the coldest of the year – of his life, which had indeed been a long one – the whole city had shut down. The snow fell harshly and heavily, the wind was relentless, the windows fought a losing battle to keep the cold outside.

It didn't help, not having heat.

The window – his basement apartment had only one – had frosted over, inside as well as out. There were laws, he thought, that should've keep his lights on at a time like this.

Once upon a time, there had been sacrifices, volcanoes and storytellers, oracles and fortune tellers, dancing girls, and so much music. He could almost, even now, hear one of those ancient rhythms. It made him smile, though the smile cracked his brittle skin and hurt.

He didn't used to feel pain.

He should have been dead. Old gods went away and died, or were overthrown, vanquished, destroyed, obliterated. Strengths faded with time. Immortality was a myth.

Yet he had survived so many thousands of years, soldiering for a time, leading bandits, hiding amongst Visigoths and barbarians and crusaders, but time proved unkind.

There were no other gods as old as he. Death, in its mercy, took them all.

Now this last old god shivered and waited for a mercy that refused to come.

He'd had his time. He'd wasted it. He never understood the ways of Change, except in the forms of music. Music always changed and grew. It was an area of expertise, of explicit joy.

Definitely, in this tiny broken apartment, enveloped by a living, breathing freeze, he heard sounds he had not heard in thousands of years. It wasn't much, three instruments only – a string, a wind, and a drum – but they were, as far as he was concerned, the original instruments, and they played the very first song.

Long ago, he had heard this song in temples and shrines and palaces. He had danced with mortals and goddesses alike, drinking wine and gorging themselves on the flesh of their lovers.

He opened his eyes. He'd been drifting, near to sleep, lulled by so impossible and familiar a song. It did not come from inside his head.

He roused himself, no easy task. He shed the blanket. His skin crackled. The blood in his veins, with reluctance, began to move.

It didn't come from outside, but upstairs.

He left his apartment, climbed the stairs out of the basement, through the ground floor and up two more flights, following the sound to a door that stood slightly ajar. Inside, there was music but also laughter, conversation, the smells of roasting meats and cheese and drink.

He was an old man now, he moved slowly and deliberately, but he had always been a god, and that's how he entered the apartment.

The party goers looked at him. The music stopped. All sounds ceased. There were ghosts among the kids – everyone was but a child by comparison, but the ghosts were as old as the god. They slipped between the children, the three musicians and all the others, whispering unintelligibly in their dead language.

"What's this?" he demanded, in the way of gods.

"A celebration," one of the ghosts said, though it used the voice of one of the modern bodies.

But the god could see the bodies of today were in a state of fear.

"Who are you?" the god asked.

"Your ghosts."

"I've never dealt in ghosts and spirits."

"Yet we have dealt in you. Now dance and sing and drink and love while you can."

The music started up again. The old god lost himself in the rhythms and the ghosts and the memories. He knew he was finally dying. It deserved a celebration. The ghosts slipped in and out of the bodies, and his body, and the old god found himself slipping between bodies himself. He tasted young flesh and renewed passion and righteousness and naïveté and wonder and fear.

He had no gifts left to give – not to the living and not to the dead – but he gave his last breath, and still, in the bodies of the young, he danced until he had exhausted them all.

Then, with his ghosts, he slipped quietly away.

23 JANUARY

The map lies.

Kenny relied on the map to get him here, to this little street that's supposed to be here, but it's not.

There's not even an alley.

No, there are two buildings butted up against each other, bricks of a similar texture and slightly different shade.

He asks a passerby, "Do you know where to find Stone Lane?"

"Sorry, no, don't know it."

He looks at the map again. There should be a Stone Lane right here leading to a cul-de-sac. It wouldn't be big or wide or anything. It should hardly be noticeable. But it shouldn't be invisible.

The buildings are both apartments or offices – the ground floor lobbies are painfully non-revealing, bland, practically barren, each fronted by a glass door, a large vestibule leading to an elevator shaft. Each has a single lift on the wall opposite the wall that should border Stone Lane.

According to the folded city map in his pocket, the road leads only to that cul-de-sac. It doesn't continue later, or cross the street. It should just be here.

He checks the map function on his phone. He says, "It should be right here."

"What should?" a woman on the street asks.

Kenny barely looks hat her. He's staring at the bricks. "Stone Lane."

"Ah," she says, and she begins to walk away.

"Wait, wait," Kenny says, running after her. "What do you mean, Ah?"

"What do you think I mean?"

"I think I must be slightly wrong, and you could correct me."

"Are you asking me something?" she asks.

"Yes," Kenny says. "Please. Where can I find Stone Lane?"

She smiles. She's pretty, though he wouldn't guess her age. She says, "On a map."

He whips the map out of his pocket. It shows Stone Lane right here. He points it out to her. He shows her the image on his phone.

"Well," she says. "Two maps say the same thing. They can't be lying to you, can they?"

"What?" Kenny asks. He blinks. "No, they can't be lying to me."

The woman shakes her head. "Perhaps your faith is misplaced. Who was the mapmaker?"

"I don't know who made the maps," Kenny admits.

"Well," she says, looking up from the map to stare at the wall. "I don't see any Stone Lane here."

"Neither do I," Kenny says. "Where is it?"

She frowns. "Haven't I answered that already?"

"I've got to be close," Kenny says.

"Oh." She shrugs. "Well, if you've got to be." She's still wearing the frown, but it's false; she's having fun at his expense.

He stuffs the map back into his pocket. He glances at his watch.

"Have you an appointment?" she asks.

"I do."

"On Stone Lane?"

"Yes."

"Are you late?"

Kenny shakes his head. "Not yet."

"Well, how much time have you got?" the woman asks.

"Maybe fifteen minutes."

"Ah, a punctual type," she says. "Maybe you're too early. Maybe it's a magic road that only appears at a specific time of day."

"Okay," Kenny says. "Thanks." He turns away.

"I'm just trying to be helpful."

"I doubt very much it's a magic road," Kenny says. A city bus stops near them, loudly, discharging passengers and picking up others.

When it's gone, the woman says, "That was my bus."

Kenny looks after it. "You missed it."

"I want to know if you find your missing street."

Kenny goes to the seam of bricks where the two buildings meet. He touches the wall. It feels just like brick.

"Maybe it's a trap street," the woman suggests. "They put those on maps to discourage dishonest cartographers. Maybe there is no Stone Lane."

" I have an appointment."

"Ah."

Kenny glances at his watch again. "In twelve minutes."

"So are you just going to stand here as the time winds down and wait for your non-magical street to suddenly appear?"

"Do you have a better idea?" Kenny asks. He's being sarcastic and mean, quite unnecessarily.

"You could perhaps search for it."

It's not an entirely stupid idea. She walks with him around the block, turning right then right then right again, but there are no other lanes or alleys or streets or roads or paths leading into this tightly packed block of buildings.

"That was useless," Kenny sighs – not a complaint about her suggestion but about the lost five minutes.

"Not entirely," she says. "You've determined, quite scientifically, it seems, that there's no entrance to Stone Lane on the outside."

"The outside?" Kenny asks.

She shrugs.

Inside both buildings, through the glass doors, he sees unadorned walls adjoining the missing street.

The glass doesn't extend to that wall in either building; he can't be sure they're back to back, that there's nothing between them. Could there be enough space for Stone Lane?

Each of the glass doors is, however, locked.

"Well," the woman says, dangling her keys. "I happen to live right here."

She unlocks one of the glass doors. They enter the vestibule. There are no doors on that side, no hallways except the one they're in. There's an elevator and a set of stairs, behind a closed door, on the other side.

"What floor are you on?" Kenny asks.

"I'm not inviting you to my place," she tells him. She returns the key to her purse.

Kenny tries the stairs. At the first landing, there's a hall. For whatever reason, the elevator doesn't stop here, but there are restrooms and a water fountain and conference rooms on that wall. The inside wall, facing the next building, has a few framed photographs and one window sill. There's no window. It's been bricked up.

"Maybe there is no more Stone Lane," the woman suggests. "Maybe they built over and through it."

Kenny glances at his watch. One minute to. "I have an appointment."

"Maybe you'd better call them."

"I can't."

"No?"

Kenny shakes his head. "I don't have a number."

"You don't have an appointment," the woman says. "Not one you're going to get to, at least."

"77 Stone Lane."

"Ah."

"There's that Ah again," Kenny says.

"You're right," she says. "There it is."

"Maybe I can get at it from the other building."

She shakes her head. "I don't have a key."

They go back downstairs. As they pass the elevator, its door slides open. No one comes out. Kenny hesitates.

"Go on," the woman says. "Seems like an invitation to me."

She follows him into the elevator. He presses the button for the Basement. When the door opens again, it's onto a poorly lit hallway. Here, the opposite wall has another bricked over window – but also a doorway.

At first, it seems locked, but it's merely wedged tight. Kenny pushes into a tiny vestibule and out through another door into a narrow alley, brick walls on three sides of him, a plaque stating Stone Lane.

It's narrow, and the bricks walls on all sides are tall. They're not unbroken, but every window seems to have been closed up, some of the brickwork is chipped or faded, the ghostly images of words – Bostonian Cigars, for instance – showing what had once been written on the sides of these buildings. There are doorways a little further in, and a cul-de-sac that's actually a courtyard, at the center of which grows a single, bare tree in a tiny plot of dirt. The woman sits on a wrought iron bench next to the tree.

"Go on," she says. "You're late."

77 Stone Lane is a small green door with a small, fading window, through which nothing is visible.

Kenny tells her, "I don't know how long I'll be."

"That's okay," she says. "If I don't wait, you can find me at number 75 Stone Lane."

24 JANUARY

One day off per month.

25 JANUARY

She faces the mirror and, quite carefully, applies her make-up – a touch of color here, a shadow there, hints and suggestions. She's brilliantly lit, perhaps harshly, by a border of lights surrounding the mirror. It's for the stage, for the actress or chorus girl or showgirl or dancer. The light highlights every possible weakness in her armor until there are none. She works diligently to make sure of it. Though the lights can be garish, the application never is. She's an expert. Despite the time she spends in the mirror, she creates neither a mask nor a façade. She accentuates and de-accentuates. She draws out her perfections, and her perfect imperfections. There's no need to hide. She's a star, even if only in her own life.

She sits at a single table among many, a row of round bulbs surrounding rectangular mirrors, but hers alone are lit. The ceiling is high, the walls far off on every side, the stage an even wider, higher, more open place than any mountain or rooftop or city hall. The stage is huge enough to handle ballet or opera or a cast of hundreds. There are five thousand empty seats, on the ground, in the mezzanine, and in the balcony. The curtains are thick and red, the wood dark and highly polished. A single spotlight shines on the stage, lighting, as yet, nothing and no one, waiting for the arrival of its star, its target, its hope. A spotlight without a star is just a circle of light.

There are no ushers, no tickets being sold, no one manning the concession stands. No one in the restroom will offer a hand towel or a fresh mint or a spray of cologne. The hall is dark. Outside, there are no posters, where once there had been posters, no promises of shows to come, no threat that you might miss something. The State Theatre's majesty is cracked and faded, and there's a wrecking ball in its future.

But not tonight.

The make-up must be powerful enough to reach the cheap seats. Everyone's paid what they can; they should get what they paid for. The orchestra pit sinks empty and hollow. When she rises from her chair before the mirror, her heels echo brilliantly on the wood floor.

It's show time. The theatre is at absolute quiet except for the echo of her footfalls. She does not hurry. She steps out from behind the curtains, onto the stage, exposed for everyone to see. She walks with confidence to the mere circle of light and fills it. She feels the thrill of expectation, the depth of desire, the unmitigated anticipation. She takes a breath.

She lets loose with the first note. It travels the length of the theatre, it reaches into the future and the past, it resonates and vibrates even as a second note is formed.

The words are old, a foreign language, but no less powerful. Each note is perfect. She loses herself to the song, as she always has. The words don't mean as much as the emotions, and the emotion is not built upon the song but expressed through it: a desperate yearning; wishes and dreams fulfilled, shattered, scattered; hope;

sorrow; hopeful sorrow and sorrowful hope. The song is merely an instrument. The message is in the notes.

When the song is over, her arms are outstretched and her head held high. She quivers. She perspires. She pants. She gave everything she had to give, and kept giving, and none of that effort was wasted.

A heartbeat before the last echo of her final note fades, the crowd erupts into applause. She bows, to this side and that side, to the center; she accepts a bouquet of roses, and other flowers are tossed onto the stage. The audience came from all times and all places, ghosts of the deceased and the living and the unborn, drawn by the simple beauty, the inescapable elegance, the overwhelming effect of her final, aching solo, unaccompanied by other musicians, one last moment of shine and glitter.

With an audible thud, the spotlight shuts down. She goes down with it, exhausted and spent, and dies with simple, undramatic quiet on the empty stage of a desolate theatre. The applause ceases, and the ghosts take their star.

In the morning, the theatre's new owner strides down the center aisle toward a stage littered by a carpet of dried flowers. His assistant follows dutifully.

The owner reaches the stage and scans the flowers. He, perhaps, hears an echo of that final aria. He takes a breath. He sees a possibility he hadn't seen before. "Cancel the wrecking ball," he tells his assistant. "I have a better idea."

26 JANUARY

It's not much of a neighborhood, but you don't exactly come here to see the sights. Killers walk these streets, and madmen, addicts that will stick you before they even know you're there. Keep your eyes open on a street like this.

It's loud, music pouring out of every briefly opened door, the sounds of pleading, the ticking of an imaginary time bomb tied directly to your heart. I'm not happy to be here, but these are my streets, I haven't got a choice, and like anybody else I've got my needs.

There's no needs this street can't fulfill.

Cassie greets me at the door. She calls me Joe. She might think it's my name. I've never seen any reason to correct her.

"Looking for some fun tonight, Joe, honey?"

I'm always looking for something. She's never really happy with my answer. She likes me, she really does, but she'll still take a twenty for ten minutes in one of those things upstairs they call a room. "Later," I promise, I'm always promising. One day, I'll take her up on her offer. But not tonight.

It's a typical club, in that it's too dark to describe with any accuracy. The clientele range from heavy hitters to college kids looking for a little something to fuel their ravenous cravings. They don't have to dance well, they just throw themselves wantonly into it and pray they survive till dawn.

The music's gothic and industrial and blood metal red. Dave's the DJ. He carts in five crates of vinyl every night. Guess he thinks it's safe enough to risk the streets, but not worth the risk of leaving them overnight.

There's a fight in one of the backrooms. There's always a fight. There's a cage and no rules. Three minute rounds until someone's laid out. No one submits. Maybe that's a rule. Far as I know, no one dies – not in the ring. Out back, I wouldn't be so sure.

There's a fight now, two guys I don't know, already bloodied, the crowd jeering them. Money's always on the line.

Through the backroom is another. Bald guy named Derek lets me in. Knows me on sight. You might call him an insurance policy. Nothing ever goes wrong in this backroom. It's all fair – or at least above board – or at least, you know what you're here for. If the business was meant to go dirty, it wouldn't be done here.

Guy behind the desk calls himself Boss. He answers to someone. I don't ask those kinds of questions. I pull an envelope from my jacket pocket and drop it on the desk. It's filled with cash. Boss won't ask where I got it and I won't tell him. It's not a game – it's that kind of business.

"Joe," Boss says, opening up his hands in a mock embrace, using them to talk as if he's Mafia. Far as I know, he's not, but I don't care.

"Three grand," I tell him.

"Yes, of course. Exactly as expected. But you're late."

"Couldn't be helped."

He smiles. It's big of him, that's what he's telling me. "What do I care, ain't that right, Joey?" He laughs. "I'm having a scotch. You want one."

I'm anxious to get what I came for, but I take the drink. Only the best for the Boss and his guests. It's tough to get the good stuff anymore. It's expensive. It survived the shipping lanes. It's also smooth. It burns my throat raw.

"I could use you," Boss says.

"I like being independent."

"I know, Joe, I know. You come and go as you please. But we've all got our vices, Joey, and I can keep you – shall we say satisfied – far better from the inside."

"You don't need a man with my particular skillset," I remind him.

"Don't sell yourself short, Joey." Boss reaches into his desk drawer and pulls out three bottles. He sets them on the desk between us. "Here you are, Joey. This is what you paid for."

His hand's still on the desk drawer. I have to lean forward to collect the black bottles. A grand each is the going price – if you can find it. You could rave for less.

He slides the drawer open as I lean in, shows me rows of bottles, perhaps two dozen. "I can make it interesting," Boss says.

I must admit, he's got my interest. Last time I saw that much ink in one place was before the war. I hesitate. You would, too. I probably lick my lips.

Boss lowers his voice. "I know what you do to get the cash. I wouldn't ask anything more from you."

"Why me?"

"Well, aren't you the best?"

I am. I don't have to tell him that.

"Tell you what," Boss says. "Keep your cash. Keep the ink. Keep all of it. Come back tomorrow night, have a go at Derek. He'll tell you what he wants. Then you can do your thing to Cassie, too, and keep her for the night."

"And there'll be others?" I ask.

"There will always be others."

I'm done hesitating. I pocket the three ink bottles, and the cash. "I can keep the rest here somewhere?"

"Already got you a room," Boss says.

I curse. I meant to keep it under my breath, but the Boss doesn't mention it.

I walk home. I don't see Cassie on my way out. It's cold, and a long, dangerous walk, but I need the air. I've got a three-room walk-up the far side of the neighborhood. Got my chair in one, and the needles, my whole kit, a half dozen pictures of my skin work on the wall.

That's not the only thing I need the ink for. In my bedroom, I've got a small desk, something of a luxury these days, and a quill. I've got plenty of blank paper – that's easier to come by than the ink – and a stack of poetry I've never shown Cassie. Maybe now I will.

27 JANUARY

Soldiers move through the trees – closing in on their target, weapons raised – in a blanket of unnatural silence. Their faces are greased, their guns cleaned, their boots encrusted with mud. They move in waves. There must be two hundred of them.

Beyond them, forming a perimeters, several Blackhawks hover – ready to fly, ready to provide support, missiles loaded and anxious for their brief freedom.

Further out, a half dozen fighter jets and a half dozen bombers and a half dozen troop carriers keep an inconspicuous distance. They fly low, so as not to be seen, and are mostly of the stealth variety, so as to avoid other forms of detection.

Off shore, there's an aircraft carrier, two battleships, and a variety of support vessels on the surface, and untold numbers of submarines beneath it.

In short, they're not taking chances.

Their target is a simple cabin. It's not unoccupied. There's a girl sitting at a table, both hands on that surface, eyes closed so she can better see. There's a boy pacing back and forth, back and forth. He's angry, frustrated, tired, hungry, cold, and frightened – same as the girl.

He says, "This is stupid."

She says, "Quiet."

The soldiers come closer. The boy goes to the window but refrains from pulling the curtain aside for a better look. They've been in these situations before. It makes him nervous. It only takes one.

He says, "Is it time yet?" He has a watch, but it only speaks of time in the ways mankind has defined it.

The girl wears no watch but she knows. She opens her eyes. She lowers her voice. She says, "Yes."

The boy smiles. It's not a joyful smile, but he no longer has to wait. He can stop pacing. He can concentrate on the job at hand. He says, "Good."

And the door opens.

The door is in the floor at the center of the cabin. You might think it leads to a cellar; in a way, and at another time, you might be right. The girl has been saying things in Latin, Babylonian, and Egyptian. She's been saying things in languages that aren't dead so much as extinct. This is in response.

The door opens and the first of the demons emerges. It's earthen toned, but its eyes burn red and it wields a sword which has, in its time, captured a thousand and one souls.

The boy's sword isn't a physical thing, but a manifestation of his strengths and talents. He swings. It shatters the demon's sword, releasing its souls, and takes the demon's head.

The second demon, bigger, scalier, with sickly yellow eyes and poisonous breath, falls just as quickly.

The third and fourth demons are twins. One wears a necklace of human fetuses. The other has a chipped tooth.

The girl says, "Watch out."

The fifth demon is bigger than the cellar door. He breaks it apart as he rises, and he roars something awful. He also screeches something awful as it joins the other four dead demons on the ground.

For a moment, it's quiet. The boy says, "That can't be all."

The girl says, "It's not."

And it isn't. The sixth, seventh, eighth, and ninth rise together. While they descend upon the boy, a useless gesture, the tenth demon goes for the girl. This is the biggest, slimiest, most vicious thing to rise from this cellar, and it swallows the girl whole before the boy can put down the other four.

The last three are smaller, but quick, lizard-like, long-tongued, fire-breathing things. Only one goes for the boy. The other two smash their way out of the cabin.

The soldiers open fire. The helicopters are called in. The twelfth demon takes a hundred rounds of ammunition before it stumbles. The boy is there to finish the job.

The thirteenth demon takes to the sky and meets the fighter jets. It takes down four before a sidewinder missile finds its way down the demon's throat. It drops to the earth with a thud. To be certain, the boy severs its head.

After the demons, a mass of the damned emerge, escaping the bowels of hell. They ignore the boy. The boy ignores them. He's tired, and they're the reason the soldiers are here. There must be a thousand crawling out of that hole. They run headlong into the soldiers, taking a rain of bullets but also taking quite a few lives in exchange. They fight for their lives and souls, though both have already been forfeited.

The boy enters the devastated cabin. There'll be men to bless and seal and send the soldiers' spirits to their eternal reward.

The girl stands by the cellar door wiping gobs of slime and mucus and gunk out of her face. There's also blood. Not hers. Nothing else comes through the door. The boy walks to the edge, looks down, sees the tenth demon retreating.

"You turned it inside out."

The girl shrugs. It doesn't much matter what she did to the thing. It won't return, and the portal has been exhausted. It's already collapsing upon itself. Quantities of demon blood will do that. When the men come to seal it, it will be permanent.

The boy says, "I'm hungry."

The girl is also. She looks at the boy and says, "You're filthy."

So they'll get showers before they eat, and maybe they'll each sleep through the night – at least until the girl locates another unsteady portal.

One day, she'll find the last of them.

28 JANUARY

Do you really want to know the secrets?

Take the magician – the illusionist, if you will. He performs, he creates tricks of mind and eye, he uses his hands and his skills to make you see a thing that isn't real and make you believe it. If he's successful, you walk away with a head full of wonder and amazement. Yet you don't go simply to have the trick pulled over your eyes – you seek the flaw, the tell, the secret. How is it done? And whether it's simple skill or elaborate trickery, when you uncover the method, the illusion is spoiled. You don't marvel at the dexterity or ingenuity. No, you walk away thinking he's a poor excuse for a magician. He let you in on the secret. The next time you see that same trick, you can say smugly to your companion, "I know how that's done. I know the truth. Here, let me spoil it for you."

I'll admit I've often been behind the scenes. I've seen the work that goes into producing a thirty minutes talk show for television. I've watched musicians argue with themselves over the inflection of a single note in a song. I've seen pencil sketches of what would later become feature length Disney animation. On the other side of that curtain, where all the ropes are being pulled, the smoke generated, the mirrors positioned, there can be a great sense of accomplishment when everything comes together and the target audience walks away without thinking of the method. When the illusion carries the day, you are successful.

Yet DVD special features, magazines, websites, friends who know or think they know, even television specials with masked magicians, will proudly reveal all the secrets that went into the creation of that illusion.

If you want to know the secrets, they are out there.

But they're not really, are they? Knowing how a thing is done is not the same as knowing how to do a thing. The revelation of a secret doesn't confer ability, not even real knowledge. If you want the secrets spoiled for you; that's your choice and you have the means. But if you want to learn the secrets, really learn them, so that you can animate your own films or create your own illusions, that requires study, practice, dedication and devotion.

It also requires sacrifice. You'll never see the illusion in the same way. But if you're sincere and earnest, if you're building a craft not just exposing its faults, you'll start to appreciate the spectacle of the creation. You'll find joy in the method and satisfaction in its execution.

Allow me to re-work my initial inquiry: Do you want to know the secrets, or do you want to be a part of creating those secrets?

29 JANUARY

The street is a snake. It slithers through the city, winding this way and that, full of venom, full of the things it's consumed. Things are people, good or bad, the snake doesn't care.

It's another Friday night. None of the lights on the snake street seem to work. There are different types of danger. Most people don't know one from another.

The snake winds around and through other streets, crossing traffic lights with cars sliding and slipping, never racing, never finding that kind of speed. Storefronts are locked tight after twilight, but there's always the clubs, the bars, the errant library, the hourly motels, the pizza places, the convenience stores.

Inside one, there's a man, big if not strong, just doing his job, answering one guy's questions as another sneaks up alongside. For a twelve pack of beer, maybe forty bucks out of the till, the secret sneaking guy takes a swing.

No one goes down. It's an awkward moment. The would-be thieves flee. The clerk, dazed, isn't sure what happened.

When his shift comes to an end, he leaves his company-issued smock and wanders the snake. He's something of a poet. He sees the beauty in the flaws and the flaws in the beauty. He thinks he knows things, but he's confused. He doesn't know what happened tonight. He stops at a bar, buys a beer, tells a girl what he knows. She's not interested. Later, when he's alone, when he doesn't know her name but knows he'll never see her again, he'll write her a poem. He'll do this in his bedroom. The window overlooks the street.

He feels the street's venom in his veins. He stops at some other convenience store for a bottle of water. He's not loyal. It's just a paycheck.

He walks in. The other two guys are here, about to do their thing, the same thing, to the girl working here. She's young and tiny, and one good fist upside her heard could be the final bite of the snake. But everything pauses when he walks in. A bell on the door announces his arrival with a tinkle. The guys pause, caught. The girls slips back, out of their trap, only now that it's too late even realizing it was there.

The fist-happy thieves glare, but he only shrugs and smiles. It's provocative. Dangerous. Like sticking your tongue out at a cobra. They're coiled tight but losing patience. He tells them, "It's not your night."

They're about to launch themselves at him, they're half an inch from lashing out, when the girl pumps her shotgun. The sound echoes over the convenience store's cheap tiled floor, bounces off stale donuts and frightening hotdogs. She announces, "We're closed."

It's enough to take the sting out of their fangs. They leave, faking nonchalance, barely able to contain themselves. When they hit the street, they run.

He goes to get his bottle of water but she swings the shotgun around. She says, "Out."

He nods once, sadly, despite a bit of thirst he's got to bite back. He doesn't have to fake calm as he leaves the shop. He's on the street again, the snake. He feels its dangerous energy through the soles of his feet. But he doesn't understand.

30 JANUARY

The temp arrived for her first day of work twenty minutes early. It was phone stuff, assisting people in doing things, which probably meant convincing people the thing they were being made to do was somehow better than they thing they wanted to do.

The temp was one in a class of twelve, though it should have been thirteen. Already, before beginning, one was lost. The instructor was a young, enthusiastic man who believed all the things he said, even if he didn't understand them.

The temp learned well. She feigned interest. It was shortly before noon before the instructor realized something was wrong. Perhaps it was the way she smiled, or the way she wore her hair. Maybe her accent. But something about her was different than any of the others, different in an uncomfortable way.

She called herself Jenny. The instructor wondered if that was her real name. Maybe it was Jennifer. Or Genevieve. Or something entirely different thanks to a witness relocation plan or because she came from a foreign country. Or another planet.

He found himself watching her in the afternoon, waiting for her to do something to justify the attention, but nothing happened. The day progressed as any other.

After a full day of instruction, the temp and all the other temps left, and the instructor stayed behind to go over tomorrow's lesson plans.

The temp was friendly, but didn't actually make friends. Who does, the first day of a new job? She went to her car and went home just as everyone else did.

He found himself thinking about the temp, this so-called Jenny. He couldn't concentrate. He went home.

The temp did not show up for the second day of instruction. It happened. One of the others also didn't come back. The instructor gave the class anyhow, and in the afternoon sent his students to listen to working agents do their thing on the phone.

The temp never came back. She didn't run into him at the supermarket or in the bookstore. He never looked over at the car next to him in traffic to see her profile.

It was her eyes, he finally decided, that he couldn't forget. They were too far apart, or too narrow, or too coppery in color. She used them well, even when just in learning. He could get used to staring into eyes like those.

Failing to find the temp in real life, he dreamt about her. He couldn't remember her voice, so she never said anything. She watched him, just as he watched her. It started to get confusing. He didn't know who was the dreamer. Who was the dream? He looked forward to sleep, knowing he might – only might, there was no guarantee – see the memory of her, catch a glimpse of an image, a reflection, an echo.

He saw her dream image when he was awake. First, in his apartment, in his kitchen, standing near the stove and staring, simply staring. He blinked, and she was gone. Then in the classroom, standing in the back of the room, watching and listening, giving him the full benefit of her eyes until he looked directly at her. She wasn't there.

Head full of wine on a Saturday night, he saw her in the parking lot standing beside his car, waiting, smiling mischievously, those eyes catching the light. But she was only mist. Smoke. A wisp of nothing, and not even that.

Eventually, he got another job in another city, packed up his apartment, and left. He hoped to leave the temp, too. But hope isn't currency. He saw her on the interstate and he saw her on the side of the road, hitching a ride, except she wasn't really there. No one was.

He met a woman in the new city and they started dating. Her eyes were arresting. She was smart and strong and excessively real. For a time, he didn't see the temp anywhere.

Then one night in a dreamt-desert, she said to him, "I'll never leave you."

"Why not?"

"You won't let me go."

As he aged, the temp did not. She was a moment of frozen time. She looked nothing like she'd actually looked, he was sure. He didn't remember her, he only remembered the memory of the temp.

He never told his wife about her. He never told his children, though she'd been there for their births. He wasn't sure if he was cheating on his wife or on the temp. He tried to convince himself he wasn't being dishonest.

In his 60s, a stroke struck him down. He couldn't see properly anymore, or think right, or speak at all. It was unpleasant from the start, and it only got worse.

The temp would visit him in the hospital, after hours, late at night, after the nurse did her rounds. She'd stare at him with those eyes. She said, "So sad."

It was a struggle to speak. "What?"

"Everything about you," she said. "I saw it from the start. You'd had dreams. What happened to them?"

"You stole them."

She shook her head. "You can't blame me. I'm not real. I'm not even a figment of your imagination. I'm a misfired synapse. I'm a faulty brainwave. You got stuck on me. I didn't stick myself to you."

He tried to apologize, but words were hard for him.

"Don't apologize," she said. "It's too late for that. Release me."

He tried to tell her he'd never had her, but his tongue refused to cooperate.

"Let me go."

He thought that would be a good thing. He had a family. A life. Something of a life.

He died in the night, wife at his side.

The temp took a long, deep breath. It was her first in almost four decades. She shook out her hair and walked out of the hospital. She disappeared in the night, swallowed by the moonlight, in search of her own dreams and the girl she'd been.

31 JANUARY

It is a big house built of dream stuff and whispers and champagne bubbles. It's at the end of a long, winding drive flanked by mythical statuary and numerous hedges and flowers and the occasional video camera, all behind ornate iron gates topped with gargoyles and barbed wire. To put it simply: one does not arrive here inadvertently, but by invitation.

A line of fancy cars and supercars and limousines lead up to the doorway. Bored chauffeurs lean against their empty vehicles smoking cigarettes and drinking cheap whisky. The good stuff's being served inside by tall, thin models and muscle-bound youths wearing dog collars.

Stephanie arrive in her sporty red BMW. She wears a mass of thin platinum strings about her neck and a gown designed by next year's top name. She ascends the stairs to the front door like a movie star, but there are actual movie stars here so almost no one seems to notice her.

"You look wonderful."

"Such a lovely display."

"Have you tried the eel?"

"Have you met the Maestro?"

It promises to be a long night. There are plenty of faces to see, and the artwork – museums' envy – on the walls, and the wandering violinists, seven or eight of them moving about like smoke on the mountain.

Stephanie accepts an offered glass of something that tastes like lost innocence. It's very sweet, and potent.

There's no reason for the party. Reasons are always over-thought. She dances briefly with a banker and listens to a poet's crude jokes. She doesn't know how to pass judgment; it's just something she does, though she never means anything by it. She hasn't yet met the host. She's not sure who's being rude, and she's not sure she cares.

Deep into the night, Stephanie finds herself on a balcony, dangling bare feet over the edge, staring out across a blue-lit swimming pool under a star-pocked sky. A violinist serenades her from the room behind her. The music shifts this way and that as the player dances, alone, in the broad library.

She reminds herself to focus. She's here for a reason, or something like a reason. Right now, this moment, as she sits, it's a frosty night in hell.

A woman steps onto the balcony. She doesn't notice Stephanie. It's a wide balcony, so it's not unforgivable. An empty wine bottle dangles from one hand, a cigarette from her mouth. Her perfectly done make-up seems garish in the soft outside light, almost clown-like, an exaggeration rather than an accent.

The woman is mumbling. She repeats the same phrase over and over as she leans over the balustrade. "Moon dragon rubies for breakfast," she says, as though it makes sense, as though the absence of those things makes her sad. She kicks off her heels and climbs.

"Maybe you shouldn't," Stephanie says.

The woman pauses, caught, exposed, suddenly uncertain. She looks at Stephanie, but she's seeing someone else – a fairy tale prince, a lover, a friend. She stands straight and says, one last time, "Moon dragon rubies."

Then she falls backwards, over the side, arms outstretched like some suicidal god.

Stephanie's on her feet in an instant, her breath disrupted, but the woman never hits the ground. There's no woman. Stephanie's alone on the balcony, alone with a melancholy violinist.

"Did you see that?" Stephanie asks. But the violinist dances away and the tempo of her song changes.

She peers over the edge, but there are only fireflies and moonlight reflected in the pool.

No, it's not only that.

There's the woman, clinging to the wall, her dress fluttering in the wind. She looks up at Stephanie. She smiles. It is not the smile of a woman. Those are not human teeth in that grin.

Stephanie steps back and away. She recognizes wrongness and wants no part of it. She finds her way blocked by the violinist. The music has stopped.

In the moonlight, the violinist's face is harsh and angular, beautiful and ugly both. Her lips are so red they're black, just like her gown, just like her eyes, which are almost completely devoid of color.

"You may be a good one," the violinist says.

Stephanie narrows her eyes. "You don't know me."

"I know enough."

The night goes quiet and dark. The moon hides behind unexpected cloudstuff. The music of the house, the chatter, the dancing, the laughter and innuendos and illicit proposals are gone, beyond reach if ever they were there.

The violinist says, "Step sideways, while you can."

It's a step away from reality, into shadow and dust and ash and mist. Stephanie steps because she's too frightened not to. She's off the path, away from the unreal house and its cars and its fancy fleshy guests. The woman laughs behind her, though the sound of her fades. The violinist is playing again.

Here, where things are strangely saturated, stark yet vibrant, uneven and unsteady, Stephanie staggers like a drunk. She sees horsemen and owls flying in formation and pearls instead of stars in the sky. She tries to steady herself, but there's nothing to grab onto. She doesn't fall. The woman laughs again.

Stephanie slips sideways and everything comes crashing back. She's alone on the balcony. She's alone in the house. The swimming pool has been emptied and the bricks are stained and weathered. No cars lines the driveway, not even her own. She sits on the front step. Slowly, the sun rises on a new day.

She's tired.

Stephanie goes back in the house. She roams the halls, she enters rooms, she opens doors, she calls out for someone, anyone, to answer.

In the backyard, under the balcony, Stephanie finds a violin. The strings are gone. It's only the body, but it's familiar. It's warm to the touch. She sits, cradling the instrument. The day proceeds without her until a girl appears on the porch. She comes walking around the side of the house.

The girl stops when she sees Stephanie. She looks nervous, but brave. "Are you the violinist?"

"Me?" Stephanie asks. "No."

"Then you're the ghost."

Stephanie smiles. "Is that the only other option?"

The girl seems confused. She doesn't answer right away. She says, "You were here that night?"

"What night?"

"The party. The wandering violinist. My grandmother used to tell me stories."

"What happened, that night?"

"You were there."

"I was."

"You are dead."

Stephanie shook her head. "I don't think so."

"But you're not the violinist."

"I don't think there ever was a violinist," Stephanie says. "I think that's a story your grandmother made up."

"My grandmother was not a liar," the girl says.

Stephanie puts down the violin and stands. "What else did she tell you?"

The girl grins. "That you should step sideways while you can." She steps closer. She carries a knife that had been hidden until that moment.

Another step away from reality, Stephanie hears the laughter and the music. When she stumbles back, she falls into the pool. No one comes to her air. She crawls out of the water and hears the violins drifting further and further away. She goes into the house, but they're all dead. Out front, the chauffeurs are dead. The woman who didn't fall when she jumped sits on the hood of Stephanie's BMW. She sees Stephanie approaching. She looks up from wiping blood from her hands with a hand towel. It's saturated. She says, "Moon dragon rubies for breakfast."

"What did you do to me?" Stephanie asks.

The woman smiles. She lays the towel beside her, covering a knife on the hood of Stephanie's two-seater. She hops off the car. She rushes Stephanie.

They tumble together onto the grass and slip sideways.

It's a long, painful moment, a clump of Stephanie's hair in one of the woman's hands, her throat in the other.

When they drop back, the cars are gone, the house dilapidated, the girl waiting with the knife. She buries it in the woman's back.

Stephanie pushes herself free of the woman's corpse. The girl smiles. She says, "That was the ghost."

Stephanie says, "Thank you."

"I didn't do it for you," the girl says. "I did it for my grandmother."

Stephanie nods. She thinks she understands. There's only one more step sideways to take, though there are no other survivors to meet her there. Except maybe the wandering violinists.

But they're long gone.

Stephanie gets into her car and drives away. The towel and knife, both blood-stained, fall off the car before she reaches the open gate and escape the eddies of a house built of dream stuff and whispers and champagne bubbles.

ABOUT THE PROJECT AND AUTHOR

InkStains is a random collection of stories – fiction and nonfiction of any genre – handwritten daily over the course of a year.

John Urbancik is a writer and photographer currently residing in the Florida panhandle. He has lived in other places and is probably best known for his fantasy, dark fantasy, and horror stories and books.

An InkStains will be released at the beginning of every month to correspond with the months in which the stories were written. The author is completing a second year concurrently with the release of these. You can follow his journey on www.darkfluidity.com.

ALSO BY JOHN URBANCIK

NOVELS
Sins of Blood and Stone
Breath of the Moon
Once Upon a Time in Midnight
DarkWalker

NOVELLAS
A Game of Colors
The Rise and Fall of Babylon (with Brian Keene)
Wings of the Butterfly
House of Shadow and Ash
Necropolis
Quicksilver
Beneath Midnight
Zombies vs. Aliens vs. Robots vs. Cowboys vs. Ninja vs.
Investment Bankers vs. Green Berets
Colette and the Tiger

COLLECTIONS
Shadows, Legends & Secrets
Sound and Vision
Tales of the Fantastic and the Phantasmagoric
(Volumes 1 and 2)

INKSTAINS